THE
ISLAND *of* HORSES

Eilís Dillon

NEW YORK REVIEW BOOKS
New York

THIS IS A NEW YORK REVIEW BOOK
PUBLISHED BY THE NEW YORK REVIEW OF BOOKS
435 Hudson St., New York, NY 10014
www.nyrb.com

The Library of Congress has cataloged the hardcover edition as follows:
Dillon, Eilís, 1920–
The Island of Horses / by Eilís Dillon.
    p. cm. — (The New York Review children's collection)
Summary: When two boys from a remote island off the Irish coast
venture to the forbidden Island of Horses, they find a beautiful and tame
black colt—and trouble with desperate men, but Pat's frail grandmother
returns with them to the island to uncover its secrets.
ISBN 1-59017-102-0 (hardcover : alk. paper)
[1. Islands—Ireland—Fiction. 2. Horses—Fiction.
3. Horse stealing—Fiction. 4. Adventure and adventurers—Fiction.
5. Mystery and detective stories. 6. Ireland—Fiction.] I. Title. II. Series.
PZ7.D5792Is 2004
[Fic]—dc22
                                              2004004449

ISBN 978-1-68137-306-5

Cover illustration: Richard Kennedy
Cover design: Leone Design, Tony Leone and Cara Ciardelli

Printed in the United States of America on acid-free paper.

1 3 5 7 9 10 8 6 4 2

CONTENTS

1

WE GO TO THE
ISLAND OF HORSES

Whenever I think of the Island of Horses now, I remember it as it looked from the boat on the first day that I landed there. All my life until then I had seen it as a darker-blue curve on the edge of the blue sea. Usually a white line of foam showed along the base of it, where the surf broke on the rocks. During storms, great cones of spray would fly into the air and drift across it like mist. We could feel their thunder, seven miles away, though we could not hear it. Then the sea and the sky were an inky, leaden black, but the island shone with a strange light like silver, and the Inishrone people would say that the wild Spanish horses were trying to land on the Island of Horses.

Inishrone is our island. It lies three miles off the coast of Connemara, nearly at the mouth of Galway Bay. Its thick end juts out into the bay, with high cliffs that save us all from being washed away by the Atlantic rollers in the wintertime. Up there on the cliffs, on a summer day, you would imagine that you could throw a stone on to the lighthouse at Bungowla, on the biggest Aran island. Inishrone is a good place, and we have a way of living that suits us, though it would not please everyone.

There are houses scattered all over the island, but there is only one village. It is called Garavin, which means bad weather. It is not well named, for it is at the sheltered side of the island, where the quay is. There are two shops there and a forge, where you can get a metal rim put on the wheel of your cart as well as have your horse shod. There is Matt Faherty's public house, where the men of the island come to drink their evening porter, and a post office run by the crankiest women in all Ireland. I do not know whether they get cranky from working in the post office or whether they are picked because they are cranky. Whatever the reason, we have had a saying on Inishrone for the last seventy years: "As cranky as the post office cat."

Our land is just west of the village, good land for potatoes and for rearing young cattle. My father and I worked it together at the time of which I speak. We kept our old pookaun below at the quay—she was a sturdy singlemasted boat, handy for a day's fishing or for taking cargo over to the mainland or in along the bay to Galway.

One sunny morning, late in April, I was down on the rough strand at Garavin, gathering weed. We had finished the spring sowing yesterday, but we were busy making a new field out of seaweed and sand to be ready for next year. It was hard work. The weed was heavy with sand and water. The slasher was blunt. The donkey was contrary, and he overturned the baskets twice before I got him off the stones. Then he grinned up at me sideways until I pulled his ears for him. I was in a fine temper with everything when I looked up and saw Pat Conroy standing at the top of the strand, laughing at me.

Pat was sixteen years old at that time, a year older and more than a head taller than myself. He was very dark-haired and dark-skinned, with deep-brown eyes and shining white teeth and an easy, good-humored look about him. When the Spaniards came in with their trawlers to shelter at our quay, they often mistook him for one of themselves. This was no wonder. We all knew that he was descended from the Spanish soldier who was washed ashore, half-drowned, at the time of the great Armada. Pat and I were good friends. Now all my ill-humor left me as I looked at him.

"Your father said to tell you not to bother bringing any more weed," he called down to me. "The Dutch captain is coming, and we should go after eels."

"I must bring this brute home first," I said. "Which boat will we take?"

"Yours. John has our own away to Rossmore."

John was Pat's elder brother. Now Pat left me to carry

the slasher while he took the donkey up the little rough path from the shore. It made me mad to see how easily he was able to guide him, with no more than a finger on those villainous, twitching ears. We went westward along the road away from the village until we came to a stony path, boreen, as we say, that led up off the road for a piece. Up there, back a little from the road, was our house.

It was one story high, like all the other houses on the island, and it had been whitewashed so often that the walls were thickly coated with glittering white lime. The thatch was held firmly in place with interlaced willow rods against the wild winter winds. At either side of the door, my mother's wallflowers filled the air with sweetness. She had decorated the edges of the little flowerbeds with whitewashed stones and the big, round, glass floats that we often found washed up on the strand after a storm. I knew that this was the most beautiful garden on the island, and I always loved the first glimpse of it as I turned in from the boreen.

We emptied the weed out of the donkey's panniers and sent him about his business.

My mother was in the kitchen when we went in. She had just baked a huge loaf of soda-bread. When she heard that we were going fishing for eels, she wrapped it in a white cloth and gave it to me. Then she filled a big bottle with buttermilk and cut four slices off the piece of bacon that was left from yesterday's dinner.

"That will keep you going for the day," she said.

"Though I don't know what good are those eels. They're like snakes. I'd as soon eat a snake any day as one of those fellows."

"As long as the captain pays good money for them, isn't it all one to us who eats them?" said Pat.

"Bring me home a fine, fat rockfish," she said, as we went off, loaded with the food and with enough good advice to take us to America.

The next place we went was to Pat's house. He lived still farther west. There was no one at home but his old grandmother when we went in. She fixed her eye on the cloth with the food in it, took her clay pipe out of her mouth, and said:

"Going after eels, I suppose. I heard the captain is coming. Watch out or the eels will bite the legs off ye."

And she burst into a delighted cackle of laughter, as if the idea pleased her. Pat went over to the dresser and took down a bowl off the top shelf. The old woman stopped laughing.

"Put that down, boy," she said softly, "or I'll tell your father where you were all Saturday evening."

Pat put the bowl down without a word. The old woman began to laugh again silently, and then she said, gasping for breath:

"Sure, take two anyway, agrá. But no more."

Pat reached up and took down the bowl again, took two eggs out of it, put them in his pocket, and replaced the bowl on the shelf. As we left the house, the grandmother called after us in a cracked screech:

"Bring me back a crab, lovey. I do like a crab."

Pat promised to look out for a crab, and then we went off, running like two wild horses down the hill to the quay. Just as we reached it, Pat remembered the eggs in his pocket. He took them out tenderly, but only one was cracked.

"How did she find out about Saturday?" I asked.

"She hears everything," said Pat. "She never stirs outside the door, and still there isn't a thing happens on the island that she doesn't know as soon as everyone else. I know who told her about Saturday, though."

"Who was it?" I asked eagerly, for I had been with him on Saturday myself, and I was not anxious to have word go home to my own people about it.

"It was Mike Coffey, of course," said Pat sourly. "Can't you imagine him sitting there opposite her on the hob of the fireplace, nursing a mug of tea and dropping tears into the ashes?" He imitated Mike's wheedling, insincere tone so that I had to laugh: " 'Oh, Mrs. Conroy, just think of the danger of it! Just picture the poor boy losing his grip and going down the face of the cliff like a stone you'd drop into the sea. And all for the sake of a few sea gulls' eggs. Oh, Mrs. Conroy, ma'am, you should tell his father, you should indeed, so that he'll put a stop to it.' "

"That's Mike, all right," said I, "but I'd say by the looks of her she's not going to tell on you. Why do you think it was Mike?"

"When we were on the ledge half-way down the face of the cliff, he sailed past within a few yards of us."

"I was too busy holding my grip to notice," I remembered.

"Then, when I got home, he was just going out the door and I coming in. The grandmother was laughing and rubbing her hands every time she'd look at me, until she went to bed. I was wondering when she'd come out with it."

He was not bitter about it. They were old sparring partners, Pat and his grandmother, but though she plagued him a good deal sometimes, they had never really fallen out with each other.

"Do you think she won't tell?" he said doubtfully.

"She doesn't like Mike no more than anyone does," I said. "She only puts up with him because he brings her the news."

Apart from his tale-bearing habits, we had our own reasons for disliking Mike Coffey. He was a frequent visitor to Inishrone. He had a big black hooker of about twenty tons, fitted out below decks like a traveling shop, with groceries, and flour and meal, and bales of cloth, and little bits of hardware and harness. He and his son Andy sailed from island to island all along the coast, from Kerry to Donegal. Andy was a long, red-haired drink of water, who never spoke above a whisper in his father's presence, though he was more than old enough to be a father himself. Mike was shorter and fatter, with grizzly gray hair in little curls, like a horny ram. He was never seen without a very flat black cap and a wide blackguardly smile that showed all his broken teeth. They had no real friends on any of the islands, as I had

heard, but they had a way of walking into the kitchen
as if they never doubted their welcome. The people were
too polite to discourage them.

Mike would sit in the most comfortable chair—he liked
a rocking chair best. He always sat with his back to the
light, so that no one could see his face too clearly. When
Mike was settled, Andy would give a little high, apologetic giggle. Then he would sit on the hob and start
warming his miserable shins at the fire. Before she would
know it, the woman of the house would be making tea
and cutting up soda-cake for the pair of them. They
always slept on the hooker at night. It was tied up to
the quay at this moment, in the choicest place by the
steps, of course. There was no sign of the Coffeys. Pat
said he thought that they were up along the island
somewhere, selling tea.

Pat had already put two barrels into our pookaun, to
bring home the eels in. There was nothing to do, then,
but to throw down our bundles by the barrels and hop in
after them. The tide was in, so that the gunwale of the
boat was just on a level with the quay wall. I pushed off
with one of the oars that we always kept lashed to the
gunwale. Pat hauled up the mainsail. In a few minutes
we were slipping out from among the other boats and
heading out to sea. Just as we rounded the quay wall, I
saw that my father had come down from the high field
where he had been working, to wave to us as we went
off.

It was a gloriously clear, sunny day. Little fat waves
slapped against the boat's sides and ran away again.

Still she sailed in a long, rolling motion that made me want to sing with delight. High overhead, the wind brushed the white clouds out like hair, so that they stretched right across the sky. When we were half a mile out from the island, heading for the long, rocky coast of the mainland, Pat lashed the helm and came to sit beside me.

"I'm sick and tired of going to the same places for eels every time," he said.

"It's the eels that decide that," said I.

I looked at him sharply then, for he was grinning up at me sideways, in the same way that the donkey did. "I don't like eels much," he went on after a pause. "And anyway, there may be eels in the place where we're going."

"Where is that?"

"To the Island of Horses. Oh, Danny, let's go there now! I've wanted to do it all my life. There's a bag of potatoes on board and plenty of turf, so we won't go hungry. We'll surely find a place to sleep there—for a couple of nights. We'll go over every inch of it. We'll climb to the top of it and look out over the whole Atlantic Ocean to America."

"But no one ever goes there," I objected after a pause. "How do we know we'll be able to land? And everyone says it's an unlucky place."

"You know that my own people used to live there, up to sixty years ago. They had boats, so there must be a quay. And if you ask me, they only say it is unlucky so that they won't have to bring the sheep out there to pasture." He grasped my arm and squeezed it until it hurt. "Danny, don't you want to go there, too? Don't you remember my grandmother's stories about what it was like when she lived there? Don't you want to find the long, silver strand and the valley of wild horses?"

On many a winter's evening, since we were small boys, Pat and I had sat in the Conroy kitchen, with no light but what came from the turf fire, and listened to the old woman's stories of the Island of Horses. She had been born and brought up there. Her family was the last to leave it. They only gave in after a winter of such storms that the roofs came off the houses, and all the old people and the cattle died, and the islanders' boats were smashed up so that they could not go for help. When the first boats went over from Inishrone in the spring, they found a little group of shivering, starving people, begging to be brought away. Not one of them had ever returned.

Pat's grandmother had been a young girl of twenty then, a dark Spanish beauty. She had married an Inishrone man, Pat's grandfather. She had settled down well enough on Inishrone, but she often annoyed the people by the way she talked about the old times on the Island of Horses. She said that the harebells were bluer and the sea pinks brighter there, and that the singers and dancers there were the finest in the whole wide world. No one could deny this. They knew that when she herself was young, as soon as she began to sing, every bird and beast on the island fell silent to listen. But now she was old, and she could sing no longer, and no one would listen to her stories except the small boys who had never heard them before.

All at once, like Pat, I found myself filled with a wild longing to go to the island. But it was no longer a hopeless wish, as it had been before. Now I had a boat, and plenty of food, and the best companion in the world to come with me.

"Of course, we'll go," I said. "I wonder why we didn't do it long ago."

It was good to feel the sadness of the last few weeks gradually blow away on the clean, fresh wind that carried us along. We had both been very dispirited, because a plan on which we had set our hearts had failed most miserably and had left us looking very foolish. This was the way it had happened.

John Conroy was Pat's elder brother, as I said before. Everyone knows that he was the finest man on Inishrone at that time. He was twenty-three years old, more than six feet tall, dark-skinned and dark-haired like Pat. He was the eldest of the family, and Pat and his two sisters, Nora and Mary, thought that the sun, moon, and stars shone out of him. Though there was no one in my family but myself, still I knew that it takes a very good man to win the love and admiration of his young brother and sisters as John had done. Wherever he was, there was sport and music and dancing. He could play the melodeon and sing every song that was ever made. He could build a coracle in two days. When he rowed in the coracle races, no other boat had a hope of winning. When he went after lobsters, he used to come home with so many that the people said he must have charmed them into the pots. And he always had a good word and a helping hand for a neighbor in time of need.

I need hardly say that such a fine man had no trouble in finding a girl willing to marry him. His choice fell on Barbara Costelloe, whose father had the big shop at Rossmore. The Inishrone people would have preferred to see him marry an island girl, of course, but still they did not grudge Barbara her good luck. We all knew her well, and everyone was prepared to welcome her to the island as soon as ever she wanted to come. They said she took after her mother, a fine, generous, big-hearted woman from Kilmurvey in the Aran Islands.

But her father, Stephen Costelloe, was a little, mean, twisted, yellow man. They used to say about him that he wanted you to pay him for walking past the door of his shop. He had a farm of good land, too, a rare thing in the neighborhood of Rossmore, and he made a bit of sour money by lending a few pounds to the people around, at a high rate of interest, for a wedding, or a funeral, or to pay taxes after a bad harvest.

The old man hated the idea of the match between John and Barbara. He said that John could only give her a poor living. He said there were four Conroys already and no room for Barbara. He wanted her to marry an old, mean man like himself, from near Clifden. You could have a bit of trust in that sort of a man, he said.

It had been Pat's idea to start a business in collecting wool from the islanders and selling it direct to a merchant in Galway. In this way he hoped to make enough money to build a new house on Inishrone for John and Barbara, so that they could snap their fingers at Stephen. There was another side to the story, too. Our people were too timid and retiring, as they still are. Mike Coffey it was who always bought their wool. When they sold it or bartered it for groceries, he gave them a mighty thin price for it. Then he sold the same wool in Galway for four or even five times the money. We were not supposed to know this, but somehow word trickled back about the great prices that were going, while we were still given the same price that was paid for wool in the year of the big famine.

Pat's idea was to sidestep Mike Coffey. He would sell the wool at the right price, take a small amount for himself out of every sale, and hand over the rest to the producers. He made many plans, but they were all modest and practical. In time, he said, he would collect the wool from all the islands, so that the business would grow from year to year. He swore that he would never grow fat and dishonest and mean as he became rich.

The next time that the Conroys were going to Galway, Pat went too. He went to see the biggest wool merchant there, Mr. Curran. He was a short, fat man, with a face like a sheep. His office smelt of oily wool. He was dressed in a black suit, Pat said, with two loops of gold chain stretched across the curve of his stomach. His clothes and his hat were covered with little bits of wool.

He did not laugh at the idea of a boy of sixteen undertaking such work, for the Conroys were a respected, industrious family. After some talk, he promised to buy any wool that Pat would bring in. Then Pat and I set about visiting every man who owned sheep on Inishrone.

It was the wrong time of the year for new wool, of course. But most of them had some that they had not bothered to sell, stowed away in lofts and sheds. They handed it over without much persuasion. What was more important still, they promised to give him the new crop, fresh and clean, when it would be sheared.

I was with Pat at every one of those interviews. Well I remember the first feeling of power and strength that flowed into us and swelled us up almost to bursting point, as we saw the plan begin to work. We baled the wool up neatly and took it in to Galway in our pookaun. When Pat was handed the price that was right for that time, we could hardly believe our eyes. The next day, full of pride, we distributed the money. Benedictions and praise followed us from door to door. One old man, Patcheen Rua from Templeaney, even recited an old prophecy to us as he put his money away in the tea caddy on the dresser. It was something about two young boys like angels of light that would arrive on horseback out of the sea and bring the good times to the islands again. All evening, by the Conroys' fire, we were purring like a couple of pet cats, while neighbors dropped in from time to time to admire us. Concealed in one of the china dogs on the mantelpiece was the seven pounds sixteen shillings and threepence that was Pat's commission.

But the next morning Mike Coffey arrived at Inish-rone. There was no question of hiding from him what had happened. In every house that he visited with his pack of groceries, the people met him with a new air of independence. Instead of ransacking the henhouse and the woolshed to pay for their purchases in kind, they handed him the money at once. Mike was not pleased at this, for he always did better on barter. Worse still, some of the people even bargained with him, to make him reduce his prices. This was a thing that had never happened before. Innocently they explained that they could afford to be more particular with him now, since they had found another way of selling their wool at far better prices. Mike sailed off that evening with a face on him as black as a June thunderstorm.

Three days later, Pat had a letter from Mr. Curran to say that he would not be able to buy any more wool from him after all. Mr. Curran said that he had spoken to the other wool merchants and that they would not be able to buy from Pat either. He gave no reasons and we never heard by what means Mike had persuaded him. Of course we knew that Mike was at the back of it, though when he came to Inishrone again a few days afterward he gave no sign of being interested in wool. He just smiled his big, toothy smile and went about his business as if nothing had happened.

Pat had raged, of course, and had sworn that he would find another buyer for the wool. But still he knew that it would be no use, and that he was not long enough in the world to know its ways. Besides, Galway is the only big town near us where any trade of this kind is done. We could not have dreamed of taking cargoes of wool along the rocky coast to Limerick or Cork in our little boats, though Pat swore that he would do this in a few years' time when he would be older. Worst of all, everyone who had encouraged and helped us before, now began to advise us to give in and admit that Mike was too clever for us.

So it was that the idea of going to the Island of Horses now seemed to us like a sign that there were still good things left in the world to do. We changed our course at once and sailed along the length of Inishrone and out past Golam Head. Here we were outside the shelter of the bay. Ours was a good boat, but she labored a little now, as she climbed and descended the dark-green waves. If one of them flicked her with its tail, I thought, she would go spinning down into the silent, dark depths of the sea like a dead fish. But then I looked at Pat and I saw that nothing could happen to us. It often happened in the old stories that a fairy boat without oars or sails would come to fetch away a hero for a visit to Tir-na-nóg. No one ever heard of the boat being lost on the way.

Still, as we approached the island, I began to see why it was that the Inishrone men never came there. It was not a stormy day, but the waves were so big that every time we slid down between two of them the island disappeared from view. From the crest of the waves I could see the good green land sloping down to the sea. It made my mouth water to look at it. But it would be madness to try bringing a batch of terrified sheep here in little boats like ours. For one thing, it could happen that, having reached the island, one would be unable to land. This put a new thought into my mind. I said:

"Pat, what will happen if the weather gets stormy and we can't leave the island again?"

I could see that he had not thought of this.

"I wouldn't mind spending a month there," he said airily, after a short pause.

Out of the corner of my eye I measured the size of the bag of potatoes and was reassured by its stoutness.

In the lee of the island the waves became a little smaller. Now we could see a short stone quay, with a blunt nose like a shark, sticking straight out into the sea. Here above all places in the world, there should have been a sheltering curve behind which a boat would be safe. They must have been a tough, wild people to have succeeded in living here at all. Even Pat was a little shaken, as I could see, at the sight of the quay.

"We'll just have to take her in as far as she'll go, without grounding her," he said.

We lowered the mainsail quickly, but she hardly seemed to slacken speed at all. For a moment I thought she would be driven high onto the rocky strand by the quay. Then, in the shallower water, she wavered. We slid her in by the quay wall. Pat grasped at the stones with his hands. Then he was up the little steps with a rope, as quick as a monkey. There were two old stone bollards there, covered with bright orange patches of lichen. I threw him another rope end and followed him.

We lashed that pookaun to the bollards as if she had been a jungle elephant and stood back panting. Then Pat began to laugh.

"I thought she was going to plow a channel up through the island," he said.

"We should have had the mainsail down from a quarter of a mile out. We'll know better next time."

We walked up the quay. Over to the right we could see a huddle of ruins, where the village had been. The walls of the little houses were rough stone, with patches of thick whitewash still clinging on here and there. Their pointed gables and windowsills were as sound as the day they were built, but there was no sign or trace of a rafter or a roof on any of them. They had all been blown away long since by the tearing winter winds. Pieces of a broken door, bleached white by the years, lay on the ground before one of the houses. Nettles and dock leaves were everywhere. We looked into some of the houses in the hope of finding a rusty pot, even, left behind when the island was deserted. But there was nothing at all. It was too long ago.

Past the houses, a flat, grass-grown track curved around by the coast. Above it were salt-bitten fields with broken walls. The island seemed to be fairly level at this end, but presently it sloped gradually upward to a high, barren, flat-topped peak. We followed the track for a piece until we came to a place where it turned upward toward the top of the island. This had been the island's main road. Pat turned at once to follow it wherever it was going, but I held him back firmly by the tail of his jersey.

"I'm not stirring another step until we get something to eat," I said. "I'm light-headed with hunger."

"So am I," he said, and he seemed disappointed, as if he had expected that the satisfaction of his longing to visit the island should have filled his stomach too.

We went back to the boat, and got out the soda-cake and the bacon, and began silently to eat. We washed them down with drafts of buttermilk, passing the bottle from hand to hand. Judging by the sun, it was about two o'clock. The quay wall gave us a little shelter from the searching wind, and we sat there quietly for a while after we had finished. Then Pat said:

"It won't do to sleep in the boat. We'd have no shelter if it rained."

There was no cabin of any kind on the pookaun. Besides, if the weather turned really stormy, she would make a mighty uneasy bed.

"Come along," I said. "I know the very place for us to camp."

2

WE HEAR THE WILD HORSES
AND CATCH SOME EELS

At the far end of the ruined village, just before the road turned uphill, I had noticed a small, square, one-roomed building. Its back was to the west wind, and its three walls were mortared solidly so that not a chink of light showed inside. Its fourth side was open. I guessed that it had been a forge long ago. It had a clean, level, earthen floor, packed so hard that even in all that time since it had been used the grass had made poor headway.

"We can easily put a roof on it," I said. "There's furze bushes in plenty up in the fields. The two oars from the boat will make rafters. We'll be as snug as if we were at home."

We each had a strong knife and a few odd pieces of string. Up in the high fields, the furze bushes glowed with deep-yellow flowers, the color of good butter. It was a joy to breathe in their sweet, wild scent. We cut branch after branch of them and tied them together at their butt ends with string, so that we could haul them down to the forge. When we had gathered a great pile of them, we went down to the boat for the oars. We carried them up on our shoulders, one each, for they were long and heavy.

Then Pat climbed up on one wall, and I handed him the oars. He laid them across, a few feet apart, and they just reached the opposite wall, so that their ends could rest there. We put stones on either end of the oars to weigh them down. Then we laid furze branches between them, big ones first, with smaller ones woven through to fill in the gaps. We had to cut a willow stick each from the clump that grew nearby to poke the branches into place. At last it was finished, and we jumped to the ground and looked at it.

"It's like a huge bird's nest," I said.

"A bird that would be a bit weak in the head," said Pat. "I don't know will it weather a storm. Maybe we should lay big stones on top of the furze, to prevent it from blowing away."

"And have them come crashing down on top of us in the middle of the night, and we asleep! That roof will hold," I said confidently. "At least as long as we'll want it."

We left a big bundle of branches by the doorway so

that we would be able to block it during the night. It had taken a long time to roof the hut, and there were still many things to be done. Though the sun was still high, the clouds had begun to turn a faint pink. The wind had got a little colder, too. We were glad that we were to be properly sheltered for the night.

We had to make several journeys up and down from the quay to the hut. We brought some turf, and an old sail, and the whole bag of potatoes. Pat insisted on this, though I thought it would have been enough to have brought up a few and to have left the bag lying there until the morning. Under the potato bag I found an old blanket that Pat had sneaked from his own home the day before, he said. I knew we were going to be glad of it. I had thought of lying on ferns and using the old sail as a coverlet, but the ferns would have been full of ticks, all mighty grateful to us for providing them with supper.

When I came up with the last load to the hut, I found that Pat had started a fire with soft, dry turf and furze branches. It smoked a great deal at first, so that I said:

"Anyone seeing that smoke will know that there is someone on the island."

"I think it's blowing away so quickly that it won't be noticed," said Pat. "Anyway we can't prevent it. We must have a fire to roast potatoes."

Pretty soon there was a little mound of glowing red ashes, and we poked the potatoes into it with our sticks.

"It will be an hour before they're cooked," I said in despair. "I can't sit here looking at them. We'll bank them over with turf and go up the road for a while until they're done."

We broke small pieces of turf and covered the mound of ashes with them so that they smoldered away finely. Then we each carved a chunk off the soda-loaf, so that we would not die of starvation before the potatoes would be cooked. Munching busily, we set out to follow the road that led uphill across the island.

For the first part it went between stone walls, where fields had been enclosed. There were rabbits everywhere, coming out to play under the slanting evening sun. They were not in the least shy of us, but sat on their haunches wriggling their little noses in that worried way that rabbits do, as they watched us pass. Presently, as the road mounted, the walls disappeared, and there were only flat, stony stretches of marshy land on either side. Here sheep would have been grazing comfortably in the old days, but now there was nothing but a couple of moorhens picking their delicate steps from one tussock of sedgy grass to another. The wind sang and whistled up here, much louder than down by the quay. After perhaps half a mile, we began to go downhill, and the fields appeared again, more hilly than before. Then the road took a turn between these hills. As we came around the bend, we both stopped, without a word, to gaze at the scene laid out before us.

This was old Mrs. Conroy's silver strand, without a doubt. Now we could see that she was right when she said it was the finest strand in the world. It faced directly out toward the west, with nothing between it and America. This was probably why all the stones had been pounded into fine silver sand. Along the whole length of its glorious curve, the long, slow waves rolled in. We knew that it must be sandy for a long way out, because the waves never broke until they were almost ashore. Then they slid back again with a wonderful, deep-singing roar, like a huge organ playing in an empty church. A little above the horizon, the setting sun sent out rays of reddish gold. Little gold-tipped clouds hung over the sea in peaceful groups, as if they were watching us quietly. Slowly and steadily the sun was going down. The sea glowed red, and everything was brighter for a few minutes. Then the wind dropped a little, and the song of the waves became louder. All at once, the sun was gone into the sea, and the whole island felt desolate and empty for the first time. Now we saw a big, dark cloud spread from the south, as if it had been watching its chance until the sun would be gone. The wind sprang up again and snarled at us meanly. At the same moment, we both found that we wanted to get back to our camp as quickly as possible.

"Up early tomorrow," said Pat. "We'll come straight here and go down to that strand. I wish we need never go home."

"Those people that lived on the island long ago," I said, as we turned and walked back by the way that we had come, "your grandmother's family, and the other families that were here—it must have hurt them sore to leave it. I wonder why they never came back in the summertime, same. I would have, if it was me."

"She was the only one that wanted to come back," said Pat. "She told me that. But she couldn't come back by herself, of course, and none of the others would come with her. She says they suffered so much in that last winter that even years afterward they used to shiver and turn white at the mention of the Island of Horses."

I wished he had not told me that. Now I felt that we were being escorted back to the ruined village by an army of ghosts. They were not malignant, but only curious. Still, they gave me the creeps.

"Come along, Pat," I shouted, "I'll race you to the camp!"

The ghosts scattered quickly from our flying feet. In a few minutes we were back at the fire, poking the potatoes out from among the ashes. They were perfectly cooked, soft and floury all through. We put more turf on the fire and made it blaze up, rather for company than for its heat, for we were fine and warm after the run. Then we sat at either side of the fire and ate our supper, cutting open the potatoes and digging out their insides with our penknives.

Before we had finished, we had both begun to yawn. We had had an exciting day, but I think we welcomed sleep also because we were beginning to be a little afraid of the solitude of our island. Neither of us said a word about this, but I know that I was mighty glad to be curled up beside Pat in the hut, before the last of the light was gone from the sky. We lay close together on the old sail, covered with the blanket. We had covered the fire with ashes and had filled up the doorway with the remaining branches of furze. There was one big gap between the branches, and presently, through this, I saw a single star. I watched it until I fell asleep.

It was pitch dark when I awoke. The star was gone. I lay very still, hoping that sleep would steal over me again. Then I began to notice what I suppose must have disturbed me. The ground under me seemed to be shaking gently. I listened with every part of me. My very hair seemed to go rigid with a terrible, primitive fear. Over and over my mind kept repeating the words: *The Island of Horses, the Island of Horses.* The shaking of the earth became a sound. There was no mistaking it. It was the sound of hoof beats on turf. With a cry of fear, I seized Pat's arm and pushed him, rattled him about until he started awake. His voice was easy and sensible.

"Danny, what is it? Don't be afraid."

"Don't you hear it? It's horses, horses galloping."

He reached out for my shoulder and held it so that I stopped trembling, while he listened. Then he said softly:

"Yes, horses galloping."

I felt him twitch the blanket aside. We got up. Still holding my shoulder, he moved toward the doorway. I went with him in a half-dream. The noise was deafening now. Ever so still we stood, hardly breathing, looking out over our barricade of furze. The sky was dark and there was no moon, but a faint grayness might have been the beginning of the dawn. Then past the hut came the horses, thundering along the grassy track. We saw nothing but a mass of flying shadows. Down past the quay they went, and along the island to the south, where we had not yet been. We listened until the sound of their hooves died away. Long after that, we were still listening, thinking that the beating of our own hearts was the drumming of hooves.

At last Pat said, with a little sigh:

"They're gone."

He dropped his hand from my shoulder. I said uneasily:

"They were real horses."

"They made enough noise for real horses," said Pat. "Tomorrow we'll find them."

We lay down again, but I could not fall asleep. Each time that I was on the edge of sleep, I would start awake again, imagining that I heard the horses returning. Beside me, Pat lay perfectly still, but I knew by his breathing that he was awake too. At last I heard him give a gentle snore, and I envied him his extra year of life, that made him so cool in the face of such astonishing things.

Presently a gray light began to show up the furze bushes in the doorway. Then the birds began their morning songs. I waited until the sun was up and then I slipped outside, without waking Pat. There had been a frost during the night, and the wind had dropped completely. The sea was a smooth, satiny, pale blue, but with a swell that crashed heavily on the stones beside the quay. All around the hut the grass was cut and torn by the galloping hooves of last night's horses. I was pleased to see it so, for I had still had a little doubt as to whether they had been real.

I poked the hot embers out from among the ashes of last night's fire and covered them with turf. Then, while I waited for it to blaze up, I went down to the quay to have a look at the boat. It could have been no more than six o'clock. The tide was out a long way, but there was just enough water at the quay to keep the boat afloat. With the way that we had lashed her to the bollards, if she had been left high and dry, she would have been hanging in mid-air now, looking mighty silly. Over to the left, I was surprised to see that there were no rocks, but a great patch of sandy mud uncovered by the tide. As I watched I saw a familiar wriggle on the edge of the sea. I went a little closer to look, and then I raced back to the hut. Pat was sitting up, rubbing his eyes.

"Eels," I shouted to him. "Millions of them! Come on!"

He was after me in a flash. He could not believe his eyes when he saw them. They lay in dozens on the surface of the water, floating helplessly. We knew, of course, that conger eels are quite helpless on a frosty morning, for we had often gone out early after them at home. But neither of us had ever seen so many of them together before.

"We must bring the boat around," said Pat.

"There's no wind," I said, "and the oars are holding up the roof of the house for us."

" 'Twould be a sin to let these eels go to waste," said Pat. "We'll have to bring the barrels down here to the edge of the water and take them in somehow. If the sun gets a bit warmer, the whole lot of them will get away on us."

We ran back to the boat. The barrels were big and heavy, made of some kind of hard wood and bound with iron hoops. We had to get a rope round each one and haul them up out of the boat on to the quay. Then we rolled them along as far as the rocky strand. Getting them over the rocks was a nightmare. Our bare feet were sore and bleeding and our hands raw by the time we had got the two barrels standing at the water's edge.

The eels were still waiting for us. The water was icy cold when we stepped into it, but we had no time to think of that. Old Mrs. Conroy's warning that the eels might bite the legs off us was no joke, as we very well knew. Pat had put an old piece of sacking and a short, thick stick into one of the barrels, and these were the whole of our gear. We each took an end of the piece of sacking, holding it wide, and slipped it under one of the milder-looking, middle-sized eels. He glared at us with his big, wicked eyes. We lifted him gently out of the water and quickly grasped the two ends of the piece of sacking together, so that he was a prisoner. He twitched and jerked, but not much, for he was still cold. Then Pat ran like a redshank with him and tipped

him into one of the barrels. He lay on the bottom of it
without stirring.

We repeated this many times, until we had almost
filled both barrels. We had lids for the barrels, with
holes punched in them, and hasps at the sides to hold
them in place. These were very necessary, because as
soon as there were several eels in the barrels they began
to get warm from contact with each other and to re-
vive. Then they started springing out of the barrels with
a strong muscular twitch of their powerful bodies. One
whack on the tail with Pat's thick stick made them helpless again. Only one eel escaped us, and we let him go.
We said he deserved his luck, but I think the real reason
was that his snapping jaws looked so terrifying that we
did not fancy tackling him while he was in his full
health. He had been the biggest of all.

At last we stood back and stretched ourselves wearily,
while we looked with satisfaction at our catch. The sun
was well up now, and the eels at the water's edge were
submerging one by one with little quick splashes.

"Just in time," said Pat. "Now we must get ropes and
moor the barrels to the rocks so that they won't be
washed away. We have no hope of getting them into
the boat. We'll have to tow them home."

With the weight of the eels inside them, we were barely
able to move the barrels at all. Still, after a lot of hard
work, we managed to get them near a big rock that
seemed to have its roots buried deeply enough in the
sand. We moored them there, with a long rope to each,
in the hope that they would float. Then we left them.

Getting them in tow with the pookaun would be another day's problem.

Back at the camp, we finished the soda-bread, and drank a great deal of fresh water from the spring well. Then we put potatoes into the hot ashes again for our next meal and tidied up the hut, for we guessed that we would spend another night there. Pat went to examine the hoofprints.

"It's hard to say how many horses there were," he said after a moment. "They were so much huddled together. I wish we could have seen them. They are not big ones, I'd say."

Sure enough, the prints looked as if they had been made by Connemara ponies. As we examined them, I thought there was something strange or wrong about them, but I could not discover what it was. An idea had flashed through my mind and was gone again before I could make head or tail of it.

"It shouldn't be hard to find them, wherever they are," Pat was saying. "We'll just follow the tracks. The island is small enough."

As we went past the head of the quay, we saw that the tide had come in a long way. Over where we had moored them, the barrels of eels were already awash. We followed the green path in the opposite direction to that which we had taken last evening. It seemed to run around by the foot of the island. The flying hooves of the horses had made such deep tracks that they were very easy to follow, even when, as happened presently, the path became partly covered in soft sand.

"Now I see what is happening," I said. "This is the proper way to the silver strand that we looked down on last night from the top of the island."

So it proved to be. About three quarters of a mile from the camp, we found ourselves at one end of the great, curving strand. Still the path ran along the top, but the tracks of the horses' hooves left it and plunged down across the sand. They spread out a little more now, as if the horses had enjoyed the freedom of the wide space. Still they remained in a group, and we thought we would now be able to guess how many had been there. But this was still impossible.

Strands are always longer than they look. Though the smooth sea never seemed more than a few yards away, we were walking for a long time before we reached it. Still the hoofprints led us on, outlined clear and hard now in the firm, wet sand. Then, all at once, both of us stopped dead. I found my voice first, to say in a half-whisper:

"Pat, those horses galloped into the sea."

3

WE FIND THE
SECRET VALLEY

Although it was broad sunlight, all of last night's terror
returned now to overwhelm me. All my life I had heard
tales about the fate that befell anyone who was bold
enough to land on the Island of Horses. Though I had
ceased to believe these stories, still I could feel now the
prickle of fear with which I had first heard them. I
could not be quite certain that the horses had not laid
this trail especially to lead us into the sea after them. I
do not believe I would have been surprised just then if
a path had opened up invitingly through the water before us. I knew that if it had I should have walked,
mesmerized, to my destruction.

It was well that Pat was with me. While I was romanc-
ing wildly, he had seen the real explanation at once.

"The tide has come up and covered their tracks
since they galloped this way," he said.

Away over at the far end of the strand the island rose
steeply and ended in a sheer cliff above the water. We
walked toward this cliff, thinking that we might find
tracks of the horses returning. But there were none.
Wherever they had gone, it was certain that they had
not come back this way.

"There is only one thing that could have happened to
them," said Pat. "It must be that there is dry ground at
the foot of that cliff at low water. That is the only way
that the horses could have left this strand."

"I wonder where they went to then?" I said.

We walked up to the top of the strand and sat down
on the rough grass to think it out.

"By the look of that tide, it will be high water about
noon," said Pat. "That will be in about two hours' time,
or a bit more, maybe. So it was low water at about six
o'clock this morning."

"And I think it was about five o'clock that the horses
galloped past the camp," I said. "You went off to sleep
again, but I didn't. It would not be much after six when
I went down to look at the boat and saw the eels. The
tide was just about on the turn that time."

"Bad luck to those eels," said Pat sourly. "Only for
them we might have followed the tracks of the horses
over here at once and then we would have been able to

go around the foot of the cliff. Well, now we must just go over the top."

And without any more discussion, we began to climb the long grassy slope from the strand to the cliff top. This part of the island seemed to be the headquarters of the rabbits. All around us there were burrows and runways, so that we had to pick our steps carefully, lest we catch our feet in a little front door. The grass was cropped as short as if a herd of sheep had been pastured there. After a while the ground became marshy, and rough sedge cut at our bare feet. Now we came upon a series of ridges, one above the other, with a deep ditch full of water below each. We had to walk along by each of these ditches until we would come to a place narrow enough to jump across.

It was slow and wearisome, and presently, when we found a dry, level spot, we lay down on our backs and had a long rest. I gazed at the sun until I was cross-eyed. Then I closed my eyes on a pink haze and listened to the sounds all around me, the singing wind high overhead, the sea gulls' cries, the busy ticking of the insects in the grass around us. Then I realized that one sound was missing. I sat up straight.

"Pat," I said, "why can't we hear the sea more clearly? We're almost at the top of the cliff. The waves should be breaking right underneath it."

He listened for a moment, and then said:

"I hear them but they are too far away."

"And I know why," I said, jumping to my feet. "We

must be on the edge of the valley of wild horses."

This had been the most wonderful part of the old woman's story. She had often told us about the hidden valley that was so hard to enter, where wild horses had lived for generation after generation since the time of the great Armada. When all the Spanish ships were scattered, in the year 1588 it was, many wrecks were cast up on the Irish coast. Day after sorrowful day, drowned bodies of men and horses came floating in on the tide. Some of the horses had succeeded in swimming ashore, small, delicate, silver-gray horses, that are said to be the ancestors of the Connemara ponies. The people caught them and kept them, and their descendants are to be seen to this day all over Connemara.

But to the Island of Horses had come a coal-black, wild-eyed stallion and a little black mare. During all of those terrible days of storm, somehow they had managed to stay together. And tied to the stallion's saddle with a gold-mounted leather belt had been a Spanish soldier. His face was like wax when they found him, so that they thought he was dead. The old woman talked about it as if she had been there herself. The gold braid of his uniform and the gold hilt of his sword were darkened with the salt sea water, she said. But presently he had revived and had stayed on the island, helping the people with their farming and fishing and breeding the wonderful jet-black horses that had given the island its name. He had not been too proud to marry an island girl, though they said there was noble blood in him.

While he had no real wish to go home, he had often

sighed for the sunny land of Spain. Within a few years
he died, and after that the stallion went wild. No one
could manage him. If an island man went near him, he
would attack with shrill screams, his forefeet pawing the
air and his mane and tail streaming out on the wind. He
took possession of the hidden valley, and the islanders
left it to him.

On the mainland in Connemara if a man owns sheep,
he leaves them wild on the mountainside to look after
themselves. From time to time he goes up and drives
down a flock of young ones, but he can never really tell
how many sheep he owns. So it came about gradually
with the wild horses. First the people were afraid of
them, and then they became lazy about them, I suppose. Whatever the reason, in the hidden valley the
wild horses lived, and the islanders would take a young
colt or filly from them now and then and break it in
either to sell or to work on the island. They were tough,
wild people themselves, as I have said, and they may
have had some sympathy with the wild horses. Very few
outsiders ever came to their island, so that the people
were not bothered with good advice and could please
themselves.

Before we reached the top of the cliff, the grass
thinned and came to an end. The last part was black-
ened limestone, bare except for a line of some pink-
flowered stonecrop a little way in from the edge. We
lay down and crawled forward to the edge to look over.
And then we were silent for a long time.

The first sight of the valley of wild horses was like a

glimpse of heaven. The cliffs dropped sheer, as if they should end in the sea, but instead, at their feet, a long, wide plain opened out. Its floor was covered with sweet, springy grass. At one side a stream of fresh water flowed down to the sea. Down there, the waves broke gently on a shelving, silvery strand. As we had guessed, the cliff on which we now lay ended over the water, but at low tide the strand would have been dry. As far as we could see, that was the only way into the valley. All the way around it, a great curve of cliffs cut it off from the rest of the island. In the face of the cliff at the far side we saw the mouths of several caves.

Even if it had been quite deserted, that valley would have been a delight. What made us lose the power of speech and movement, so that we could do nothing but gaze and gaze downward, was the glorious moving pattern of galloping horses. There were about thirty of them, though we did not count them then. Most of them were silver-gray Connemara ponies, but there were some bays and blacks as well. Their leader was a wild black stallion, who might have been the direct descendant of the little black warhorse that swam ashore here so many years ago. With arched neck and sweeping mane and tail, he wheeled and circled. When he jumped the stream, they all followed. When he stopped for a moment, so did they. As we watched them, we began to notice that several of the black mares had foals running at their sides. The blacks looked in a strange way wilder and happier than the rest. It was something in the way they tossed their heads and threw their hooves out sideways as they cantered about.

Presently the leader paused and began to crop the grass. Then the whole scene became slow and peaceful. The warmth of the sun on our backs, the soft music of the waves, and the gentle, easy movement of the horses, all combined to make us drowsy with contentment. At last Pat spoke, and his voice was heavy, as if he were talking in his sleep.

"I wish we could stay here forever. I wish we need never go home." After another pause he went on: "We'll come here every summer. We'll sleep in the hut and spend days and days here with the horses."

Then he stopped. I made no reply. There was no need for either of us to say what was in our minds. Already, on Inishrone, our work was valued as the work of men. Every year until now, as soon as the potatoes were planted, we had a few weeks that were our own. We could lie hour after hour in the old fort at the top of the island, talking and planning, or we could go off every day fishing, if the weather was good, only driven home at last by the cold or by the hunger. But this year, though nothing had been said, a part of the work had always been left for us to do. We knew that if we went off to amuse ourselves, the work would lie there undone, waiting for our return. Then Pat said:

"We could start bringing sheep here to graze. That would give us an excuse for coming."

"But you know what would happen then," I said.

"Someone would find out about the horses, and the next thing they would be out with boats, catching them and bringing them home."

"True enough. We'd best say nothing about them."

There and then, we nearly burst with the thought of keeping such a secret to ourselves. After a moment I said:

"Are we going to climb down into the valley?"

"I think we should wait until the tide goes down again," said Pat, "and go around by the strand. Supposing one of us fell down that cliff, the other one would have a fine job getting him out again."

This was so sensible that I had to agree to wait. The sight of the horses galloping so wild and free had aroused a wish in us to do the same. We bounded down the side of the hill, leaping from tussock to tussock like hares in long grass. We hardly noticed the ditches and the rabbit holes this time. We tumbled head over heels and shouted when we reached the grassy path from the strand. We threw ourselves on the grass by our fire at last and lay there, panting.

The next few hours were like to kill us. We ate our potatoes, and made up the fire, and put more potatoes to roast. We visited our eels so often that they must have been heartily tired of us. The barrels were floating, rising and falling gently on the waves. We went for a swim by the quay, to cool our excitement. The water was sharply cold, and I think it did help to make the waiting possible. Then, for a long time, we sat on the quay and watched the pookaun drop slowly lower and lower as the tide went down. At last I said:

"Now we can go."

Without a word, we started back to the silver strand. The afternoon was already turning cool, although it was not much later than three o'clock. The sea was a little rougher than it had been, and it had a greenish look about it that I did not like. Still, the sky was clear enough. Although it was only a few hours since we had talked cheerfully of spending the summer here, we were both getting a little uneasy at the length of time that we had stayed away from home. If a storm came up now, as I well knew, it might easily be several weeks before we could leave the island.

When we reached the strand, the tide was much lower than it had been in the morning. As we went toward it, we could see that the cliff now rose out of dry, firm sand.

"We could have brought the boat around here hours ago," I said, but Pat thought that this would have been foolish.

"Besides," he said calmly, "it will be easier to get the colt into the boat from the quay."

"The small black one with the light feet?"

"Of course. Oh, Danny, he's the king of them all! I can't go home without him."

"He's the king of them all, without a doubt," I said slowly. "I couldn't take my eyes off him either. But I'm thinking we'll be in trouble if we bring him home. The people will want to know where we got him."

"We'll say we found him," said Pat airily. "Besides,
who has a better right to him than me? It's as plain as
a pikestaff that he's descended from the old Spanish
stallion. No one denies that I'm descended from the
stallion's owner. I'll give him to John. If John were to
promise Stephen a present of that colt, it might soften
him out and stop his complaining."

This was such a good reason for bringing home the
colt that I made no more objections. There was no better
judge of a horse in the whole country than Stephen
Costelloe, and I knew that when he would see the colt
he would not be long in deciding between it and Barbara.
Part of his meanness was that he had to have the best
of everything for himself.

We rounded the end of the cliff and walked up the
strand. When we reached the grassy floor of the valley
we went more slowly so as not to frighten the horses. As
we approached them, they lifted their heads in that
quick way that horses have. They looked at us steadily,
but they did not run away.

"They have never seen people before, I suppose," said
Pat.

It was wonderful to walk up to them as they drank
out of the stream or grazed peacefully and stroke their
necks until their ears twitched with pleasure. Only the
blacks were a little suspicious of us. The older ones
sidled away and would not let us touch them. We let
them alone, for we knew that if they fought us for possession of the colt, they would be sure to win the battle.

The colt was no more than seven or eight months old.

His skin shone like the black satin bands on my mother's best skirt. His legs were so straight and slender that you wondered how they could hold him up at all, and his little round hooves shone like stones newly washed by the sea. He turned his long arched neck to look at us. There was such intelligence and understanding in his eyes that I said in a low voice:

"It's like taking a child from its mother, Pat."

"I can't go home without him," Pat repeated after a moment.

He put out his hand slowly and stroked the colt's neck. The colt shivered once and then moved closer to him. Very gently, we began to walk back to the strand, with the colt walking peacefully between us. He swished his long tail and seemed quite content. We kept our eyes on the other horses, but they took no notice of our departure. They had already gone back to their own pursuits.

Still, we were uneasy until we had rounded the end of the cliff and were crossing the silver strand. All the way back to the camp we kept looking fearfully behind us. We never stopped until we had the colt safely stabled in the hut. Then we blocked the door with furze bushes as best we could and sat down to eat our supper by the fire.

4

WE BRING HOME
THE COLT

We did not leave the camp again that night. By the time we had finished eating, the dusk was beginning to fall. There had been no warmth in the yellow sunset. Now the sky was heavily clouded over, and it was wretchedly cold. Still our spirits were high as we covered the fire and prepared to sleep in the hut for the last time.

It was not easy to persuade the colt to lie down. He stood with his legs immovably apart for a long time, but at last, by stroking and coaxing, we got him folded up neatly in a corner of the hut. We spread the old sail beside him, and I lay down on it. But Pat leaned against the colt, with one arm around his neck.

"I'm going to sleep like this," he said. "It's the only

way I can be sure he won't go away in the night unknown to us."

It was easier to go to sleep this second night. We were tired enough to forget that the ground was hard and cold, and we hardly heard the mean little wind moaning like a sick banshee around the hut. Before the last light had entirely left the sky we were fast asleep.

It was still pitch dark when I awoke to feel Pat shaking me.

"The colt!" he gasped. "Help me to hold him."

All around, just as before, the ground was shaking and the night was loud with the drumming of hooves.

"What is it?" I said stupidly.

"It's the wild horses coming again, and if we don't hold him this fellow will be off with them."

Feeling for him in the dark with my hands, I discovered that the colt was standing up now. Little quick shivers went through him. I ran my hand up his neck to his head and found his ears poked hard forward. Then we heard a wild, shrill, quivering squeal outside.

"That's the black stallion!" whispered Pat.

We clung to the colt's neck as he began to plunge forward. He kicked his hind legs high in the air and tossed his head, trying to shake us off. His hooves struck the walls of the hut. The stallion squealed again, and the colt whinnied a reply.

"If that stallion comes looking for us, we're finished," said Pat in a low voice. "Hang on tight and this lad will get tired of struggling."

We dared not relax our hold for a moment to look out

through the doorway. By the sounds we knew that the horses had not paused in their wild flight. Then, away off in the distance, we heard the stallion again. As if he knew that they had deserted him, the colt stood still now, with only an occasional long shiver to betray his excitement. At last, when we could no longer hear the wild horses, we persuaded him to lie down again. But we got no more sleep that night. In the hour that remained before the dawn we lay closely against him, talking gently to him and to each other.

Presently we could see the outline of the furze bushes against the sky. Then the grayness became white, and gradually it was morning. Still we did not move, because we knew that while the tide was out the wild horses could come again. We munched the last hard crusts of to soda-bread that we had brought with us and sucked the raw eggs because we did not want to go outside to cook them.

It must have been almost eight o'clock when I stepped out into the sunlight at last. The wind had lightened a little. Rags of cloud were tossed around in a blue sky, and though the sea was dark blue, it had a ruffled, heavy look about it.

"I think we could let him out to graze for a while now," I called out to Pat. "And he must be wanting a drink, too."

I ran down and got a rope off the boat to make a headstall for the colt. Then Pat took him to the stream that flowed out of the spring well, and he had a long drink. When I left him, the colt was grazing peacefully at the end of his rope, and Pat was watching him like a mother with an only child.

Down at the boat again, I began to work out how we would get the colt on board. The easiest way to bring him back to Inishrone might have been to let him swim after the boat at the end of a rope. But he was too young, and the distance was too long to risk this. A pookaun is not a big boat, but since there was no cabin of any kind in her, there would be plenty of room for the colt to stand or lie down. Our main problem, I thought, would be to keep him quiet.

The ballast, of stones, was laid out like a neat paving on the bottom of the boat. Now I cleared this of the various bits of gear that were lying about on it. Then I pulled some soft green grass and spread it out, so that the stones would not hurt his feet. Then, still leaving Pat to mind the colt, I brought down the old sail, the blanket, and the remains of the bag of potatoes, and stowed them in the stern. I climbed the wall of our hut and pulled away first one oar and then the other. The furze branches fell softly on to the floor inside.

At last, when I had everything ready, I said to Pat:

"Now we have only to get his worship, there, on board, and we can be off home."

Pat was nuzzling at the colt as if he were another.

"This fellow will do whatever I tell him," he said. "Come along, old friend, and we'll take you sailing."

But at the quay Pat stopped suddenly in his tracks.

"The crab!" he said. "The crab for my grandmother. I nearly forgot it. Here, hold this lad a while till I go after one."

A moment later he was skipping over the rocks by the side of the quay, down past the slob land where we had caught the eels. I saw him hang, head downward, from a big flat rock that jutted over a sea-water pool. Then suddenly his hand darted into the water. When he withdrew it, I could see that he had a stout little crab, firmly grasped by the back of its shell, waving its slow, silly feelers helplessly in the air. He was back at the quay in a moment, stowing the crab in the fish box in the stern of the pookaun. Then he stood at the gunwale, at the foot of the steps, and said:

"Now, Danny, just lead him down here to me."

And that was exactly what I did. At the top of the steps the colt stopped and seemed to dig his hooves into the ground in that exasperating way that horses have. Pat reached out his hands to him, as you might call a child. The colt looked down into the boat, for all the world as if he were wondering whether it was seaworthy. Then, very cautiously, feeling every step with his hooves, he followed me down to the boat. Then he gathered himself together and boarded her with a quick little spring. For a moment it looked as if he might spring right back on to the dry land again. His eyes rolled wildly, and his head came up with a jerk. But then he seemed to decide that it would be easier to stay where he was. When I saw him balance his legs against the rise and fall of the pookaun, I knew that we had him safe.

We had not forgotten the eels. It was too much to expect that the colt would lie down, and since he seemed to like Pat better than me, I left them together. I took a long rope with me and a big cork float, for our plan was to use the rising tide to help us to take the barrels in tow.

The barrels were still high and dry, but by this time they were no more than four feet from the water's edge. First I tied the two of them together with the rope with which they had been moored to the rocks. Then I took my new piece and tied it to the connecting rope, with a special knot that my father had shown me. Lastly I tied the float firmly to the end of the rope and flung it as far out to sea as I could. The float bobbed up and down quietly, outside the line of small breakers.

Back in the boat, Pat said:

"That will work fine if the float is not washed up on the strand."

"If it is, I'll have to swim in for it," I said resignedly.

Though I was a good swimmer, I believed then as I do now that the sea was made for fish and not for people. The Atlantic Ocean is a mighty cold bath in the month of April, as we had proved yesterday.

We sat there in the boat for a while, watching each wave move an inch nearer to the barrels. It was almost an hour before we saw them lift gently on the tide. Then we cast off as quietly as we could, so as not to frighten the colt. He seemed to have become quite accustomed to the pookaun, however, and gave us no trouble. Still we were afraid that if the boat gave a sudden lurch he would take fright and jump overboard to swim for home.

In case this should happen, I tied the trailing end of his headstall to the gunwale. Then, as we sailed along the line of the shore, Pat stroked him and petted him. The boom just cleared his head every time it swung over, but we soon found that this had the effect of making him cower down to safety.

I did not have to go for a swim after all. We picked up the float quite easily, and I hauled the barrels toward us until we had them trailing after us on a short rope. And now at last we were able to set out for home.

That was an uneasy journey. We had a following sea, and the stern of the boat could not lift to it as it should, because of the weight of the barrels of eels. It was almost as if the boat were half full of water. Then I had to attend to the sails single-handed, because Pat dared not take his hand off the colt for as much as one moment. To begin with, we had thought that it would be no great matter if the colt jumped overboard and had to swim after us. But when we saw the heavy, dark waves chasing us and felt the slow drag of the pookaun under us, we began to think that the colt's leap overboard might be enough to capsize the boat. If that happened, none of us would ever be heard of again. For every yard of that seven miles home Pat kept one hand on the colt's wild head, while he talked to him gently.

We had forgotten to cook some potatoes for the

journey. There had been too many other things to think of. We found an old rusty tin of water among the gear, but when I saw that a colony of little wriggling beasts had taken up lodging in the bottom of it, I handed it silently to the colt. He put his soft nose down into the tin and drank up the contents, to the last astonished wriggler.

"It must be grand not to be too particular," said Pat enviously, as he watched the colt smack his lips with enjoyment.

From time to time we looked back at the island. Immediately we left it, the outline and color of it began to change slowly back to what they had been before ever we had landed there. The high green hill became a dark-blue curve. The breaking waves became a silent white line. Presently the quay disappeared, and then the whole island was once more the mysterious, remote picture that it had been for me as long as I could remember. It was so different from the place where we had spent the last two days that I could almost have imagined that I had dreamed myself into one of the pictures on our kitchen wall, as I used to do in idle moments when I was a small boy.

But there was Pat to prove that it was all true, and there was the colt and the two barrels of eels. In any case, as we approached Inishrone, we had too many other things to think of to be lonesome for the Island of Horses.

"Mike Coffey's boat is still there," said Pat. "I was hoping he'd be gone when we'd get back."

"And the Dutch captain is here," I said as we came nearer.

His stumpy, gray boat was moored in deep water at the end of the quay. The Dutch captain had a name, but no one could remember it. He was stumpy and gray like his boat. He was almost completely bald, as you could see when he took off his peaked cap. He was very polite, and he used to sit in the kitchen with his cap on his knee, while the children of the house would gather around to wonder at him. He was always dressed in a black seaman's jersey and black trousers, held up by a broad, black leather belt around his wide middle. He had large, comfortable, brown eyes like a seal. No one on the island knew a word of his language, and he did not know a word of ours. Still we managed to sell him lobsters and eels. He seemed to like Inishrone, and he often stayed on for a day or two after he had finished his business, sitting on the quay wall in the sun. He usually had an island boy working on the boat with him. At that time it was a boy called Brian O'Donnell from Templebreedy, at the other end of the island. He was the envy of us all, with his stories of the foreign ports that he had visited and the queer, wonderful things that he had seen.

Just outside the quay, I let down a line and caught a rockfish for my mother. The colt hated that fish, for some reason. For the first time since we had left the Island of Horses he pranced and kicked. Pat held him short by the mouth while I lowered the mainsail and brought the boat around to the quay single-handed. We were so busy that we were almost in before we noticed that half the men of Garavin were standing on the quay waiting for us.

My father was there and Pat's father, Bartley Conroy. They looked us over sharply to see that we were not missing an arm or a leg after our two days' absence. Then all the men took charge of the boat, and we were very glad of their help. They moored the pookaun for us, and got the colt ashore, and the two barrels of eels. Matt Faherty, from the public house, was infatuated with the colt.

"Isn't he the beauty! Oh, isn't he the wonder to the world!" he said over and over again.

"Where did you get him?" my father asked.

"We found him swimming," said Pat without a blush.

"Did you so?" said Derry Folan, the blacksmith. He looked at the colt's hooves with a professional eye. "He's never been shod."

Immediately I remembered what it was that had run through my mind on the island. The thought had fled away again so quickly that I had not recaptured it until now. I was so astonished that I was quite unable to speak. Fortunately no one was taking any notice of me just then, for they were all examining the colt.

"Maybe he'll make your fortune, like Clancy's goose," said Tom Kenny, who owned the next farm to ours.

There was a burst of laughter at this. The Clancy family was huge and very poor, but not at all disorderly. It was kept going largely by contributions from the neighbors. At eleven o'clock on any morning a Clancy

child might pad bare-footed into the kitchen. Silently
a bottle would be extended for milk, or a whispering
voice would ask for the loan of a few eggs, or some flour
to make a cake, or an onion to go with the potatoes. It
was always called a loan, though none of these things
had ever been known to be returned. Still the people did
not mind. The woman of the house would always cut a
big slice of bread for the child and give whatever was
asked for, in the name of God. Then the child would
scuttle out, still silently, and hop over the walls home,
like a swallow on a wet day. Six of them would run into
their mother's house almost at the same moment, with
different pieces of loot. They were always very poorly
dressed. We used to be told that this was all because their
father was a sailor instead of a farmer.

Then, two years ago, one of the Clancy children had
found a goose on the strand. Being well trained, he had
got it up in his arms somehow and had brought it home
to his mother. She was an honest poor woman, and she
had visited every house on Inishrone, asking if anyone
had lost a goose. No one had, and at last a conference
of the islanders had agreed that she should keep it.

Mrs. Clancy did not own as much land as would sod
a lark, as we say. She had grazed the goose with a
neighbor's flock. Presently it had laid eggs and reared a
brood of goslings. With the money that she got for the
goslings at Christmas, she had bought a ewe lamb in
March. Another neighbor had given her the grazing
of the lamb, which was now full grown and the mother

of twin ewe lambs. In this way, Mrs. Clancy was in a fair way to becoming a farmer.

While the men had been discussing the colt, the Dutch captain had been silently opening the barrels of eels. He gave a sharp cry when he saw the size and the number of them, so that several of the men came over to look.

"Where did you get those monsters?" asked Matt Faherty after a moment.

"Out by Golam Head," said Pat. "They were lying on top of the water after the frost in the early morning. 'Twas the easiest thing in the world to take them in."

The last part of this statement was true, at any rate. Everyone watched while the Dutch captain emptied the barrels of eels into his boat. He paid us for them at once, and we divided the money between us. As I slipped my share into my pocket, I felt a hand on my shoulder, too hearty to be sincere. Before I turned around I knew that it could be no one but Mike Coffey. As I thought, the sight of the money going into my pocket was giving him agonizing pain. Now his sticky-sweet voice sounded in my ear:

"Ah, isn't it a fine thing to see two young lads so hardy. Won't your mother be the proud woman when you hand her over that money." He dragged the word out lovingly. "But do you know what she would like better still?"

"What's that?" I asked suspiciously.

"Just what I have here for you."

Quickly he twitched from behind his back, where he had been holding it in readiness, a little bolt of pale-blue cotton scattered with daisies. He saw in a flash that I thought it was beautiful and that I was turning over in my mind whether I would buy it or not. I knew that my mother loved a pretty flowered apron better than anything in the world. Whenever she had a new one, I would see her stroking it gently and admiring it when she thought no one was looking.

"Take it in your hand," Mike was saying softly. "Go on. Hold it. Feel it. There's nothing a woman likes better than a piece of flowery cloth."

If he had not said that, I might have bought it. He had not been able entirely to conceal the contempt that he felt for his ignorant customers.

"Thanks," I said. "I'd rather let her choose it herself. I'd like to be sure she was pleased."

"And are you going to go home to your mother with one hand as long as the other?" he said, in mock horror.

"I have the eel money for her," I pointed out, "and a rockfish besides. She'll like that fine."

He saw that he had to be contented with this, and he went off with his piece of cloth.

"The young people nowadays have no nature in them," he said, with a windy sigh.

With my eyes on the beautiful bolt of cloth, I watched him move away. Then I noticed my father watching me with an approving grin.

"I think I reared you well, Danny," he said. "That

same piece of cloth is over in Stephen Costelloe's shop in Rossmore, sixpence a yard cheaper."

"Of course, a colt is not like a goose," Derry Folan was saying. "You'll have to keep him for a while until you see will anyone claim him."

"I'll do that," said Pat confidently.

He picked up his grandmother's crab with one hand and took the colt's headstall with the other. I took my rockfish by the gills, and we started up the quay. The colt lifted his feet delicately on the stony road. It was good to be at home again in the sunny, windblown evening. Some of the men left us at the village, and some walked west along the road with us until we came to our house. There we all promised to go over to the Conroys' for the evening, and my father and I turned in home.

5

WE HEAR FROM MIKE COFFEY

My mother had heard that we were at the quay, and she had a feast ready that more than made up for my two days of short rations. She was delighted with her rockfish, and she commended me for my refusal to buy the apron stuff from Mike Coffey. Still I made her promise to buy some the next time she would be in Rossmore. I washed down the last potato cake with a huge mug of buttermilk. My father said:

"And wait till you see the black colt that Patcheen Conroy has. They brought him home standing in the pookaun. He was just getting a bit cross, though, when they reached the quay."

"Where did you get him?" my mother asked.

"Swimming," I answered, remembering Pat's word.
"Where?" my mother persisted quietly.
"Out by Golam Head," I stammered.

I was never any good to tell a yarn, especially to my mother. I could see now that she had her doubts about me, and I was mighty relieved when she dropped the subject. I resolved to talk the whole question over with Pat and persuade him to agree that we tell our parents the true story of the colt. It was small comfort to know that we were honest if my own mother doubted it. Besides, there was the other idea that I wanted to discuss with Pat, which made me wonder if my mother might not be right, after all.

As soon as I had finished, my father and I went to milk our two black Kerry cows. They were in a field near the house, and we milked them there without driving them in. I was glad of this, for if we had been close together in the cow stable there would surely have been more talk of the colt. I did not know how long it would be before my father would begin to see the various flaws in our story. Just now, I was almost too tired to worry about that. Potato cakes always made me sleepy. It was pleasant out in the fields under the evening sun, with the short, cool grass under my bare knee as I knelt down to milk the cow. She swished her feathery tail slowly, but though she grinned to herself, she did not hit me with it this evening.

We brought home our buckets of milk and distributed the contents. Some went into the tall churn to make butter. Some was put aside for drinking and to put into tea. Some went into the big barrel for the pigs. By the time we had finished, my mother had washed up the supper things and had shut in the hens for the night. Then she took her Sunday shawl from behind the door, and we were ready to go to Conroys' house.

The kitchen was crowded when we arrived. It was the best kitchen on the island for a dance, and I could see that there was going to be one tonight. Pat's sisters, Nora and Mary, were moving the lustre jugs from the lower shelves of the dresser to the upper ones. The butter dish, in the shape of a brown glass hen sitting on a nest, had been put on the mantel shelf between the china dogs and the photographs of the aunts in America. The big table had been moved out into the back kitchen, where some of the older men had already gathered to talk. The kitchen chairs were ranged around the walls.

John was sitting on one hob of the fireplace, trying a tune out on the melodeon. I looked around for Pat, and saw that he had drawn up a low stool, creepies we call them, by the opposite hob, where the grandmother always sat. She was cackling with laughter, swaying up and down, but I could not hear what Pat was saying to her, with the noise of all the people and the melodeon.

Pat's mother took my mother away into a corner for a chat. My father joined the group of older men and I was left alone. I edged around toward the fireplace. The Dutch captain was sitting in the rocking chair next to Pat, swinging gently up and down and smiling happily to himself as he watched the dancers get ready for the first set. Just as John played the opening bars of

"The Connaughtman's Rambles," I saw Mike Coffey appear in the doorway. His eye lit on the rocking chair at once. When he saw that it was already occupied, his face wrinkled up with hatred, like the top of a jug of sour milk. The Dutch captain took no notice. It was clear that he planned to spend the whole evening in that rocking chair, swinging gently up and down and smoking his long-stemmed pipe.

As soon as I caught Pat's eye, I jerked my head, ever so slightly, toward the back door. He nodded, in the middle of his account of our capture of the eels. The dance was in full swing now. I slipped around behind the backs of the spectators until I came to the back kitchen. The men did not lift their heads as I passed through, for they were so busy talking.

It was still light outside. I leaned against the gable end of the house to wait for Pat. From this height, I could look down toward Templebreedy, the village at the end of the island. There was a reef of rocks there and a lighthouse to warn the ships away. Already the light was winking peacefully at the calm sea. Away out on the horizon, I could just see the outline of the Island of Horses.

When Pat appeared, we strolled down the short path to the road and sat on the grassy edge just at the cross. Though this was a regular meeting place for the men, there was no one here tonight but ourselves. Still I looked around to make sure that we were alone before I said:

"Pat, I think we should tell where we got the colt."

He looked shocked. "Is it tell the world?"

"No, no. But you tell your father and I'll tell mine."

"You must have a reason for that idea," said Pat. As I hesitated while I tried to find words, he went on eagerly: "Didn't we agree that we'd tell no one, for fear they'd all be out with the boats to catch the horses and bring them home? Didn't we say that the Island of Horses would be our island, where no one would ever go but the two of us only?"

"Other people do go there," I said sharply.

"Who goes there? What have you heard?"

"I've heard nothing. But some of the horses had been shod."

He was silent for so long that I put out my hand at last and shook him gently. Then he said, in a miserable whisper:

"Oh, Danny, isn't it a terrible thing to be as big a fool as I am? When did you notice it?"

I knew that the thought of the colt not being his own after all was stinging him like a hundred bees. I tried to keep my voice easy as I answered:

"I half-noticed it when we came out of the hut on the first morning and saw the hoof prints all around us. It was just that I thought there was something strange about them, but I couldn't put a name to it. Then when Derry Folan remarked below at the quay that the colt had never been shod, it came back to me all at once. The colt was never shod, right enough, but some of the others must have been."

"It beats me," said Pat, and then we were silent, thinking about it, for a long time.

We might have sat there until dawn if we had not been disturbed by a heavy footstep on the boreen down from Conroys' house. I twisted around and peered into the dusk. Then came Mike Coffey's hard, jovial voice. He had seen us without any difficulty.

"Ah, there you are, to be sure. Young lads never care for dancing."

He got out an old checkered handkerchief and laid it carefully on the grass beside me. Then he sat down, stiff-jointedly, on the handkerchief. He was so clearly trying to be friendly that I wondered at what moment he would produce something from his pocket for us to buy. I guessed he had not so easily forgotten the good money that he had seen us handle a short time ago.

He leaned back against the grassy bank with his hands behind his head, trying to look as if this was his favorite position.

"That was a very successful excursion for the pair of you," he said admiringly. "I'd say your mothers were proud of you when you got in home."

He's coming to the money now, thought I. But he went on:

"Tell me, did either of your mothers ask you where you got the colt?"

So he wants to buy the colt, I thought, as I replied: "Mine did."

Pat sat perfectly still beside me, so that I almost doubted whether he was listening. Mike said:

"And what did you tell her?"

"What we told you, of course."

"That you found him swimming," said Mike thoughtfully. "It was a good story. Nothing given away. Just— swimming. But if you wanted anyone to believe that, you should have put the colt into the sea, so that he would have been wet."

"There was plenty of time for him to get dry," I said weakly enough.

"Ah, but it takes a long time for a really wet horse to get dry," said Mike. "And another thing: it would be very hard for two young lads to get even a little colt like that up out of the sea and into a pookaun. Indeed I don't see how it could be done at all, without wrecking the boat."

"He was glad to come on board. He was tired from swimming."

At the other side of me, I could feel Pat nudge me with his elbow. I guessed that he was warning me against giving too many details.

"Do you tell me that he climbed on board by himself?" Mike asked in mock astonishment.

"I did not say that," I shouted.

"Now, now! Let us not be angry." He laid a hand on my arm. It was all I could do not to knock it off. He withdrew it after a moment and went on: "And where did you find the eels?"

"What business is that of yours?" I asked rudely.

We could have got up and run away, of course, but somehow it did not occur to us to do this. I think it was curiosity as to what Mike would say next that held us. He was not in the least disturbed at my outburst.

"I take an interest in eels," he said easily. "The Templebreedy men were over at Golam Head after eels yesterday, and there were none there."

I was silent at this. I knew that news of our catch would be all over the island by now. It would not be long until one of the Templebreedy men would be in at our door, chatting to my father about eels and mentioning that they had come back with empty barrels from the very same place where we had filled ours. I wished Mike would leave us, so that I could go back to Conroys' and fetch out my father and tell him the whole story.

At this point we heard a high, wild giggle, like a horse's whinny, and there was Mike's son Andy chattering and gibbering while he sat down awkwardly beside his father.

"There you are, father, there you are. You found the lads, you found them, you did indeed."

"Sit down and hold your tongue," said Mike with cold venom.

Andy gave a little trembling wail, which he cut off short at the end as if he had been strangled suddenly. Andy sat down in a spidery heap and was silent.

"I know where you were, you see," Mike said to us casually. "You were on the Island of Horses."

There was a long silence. Andy sat up and peered into our faces, to see how we were taking this. His father pushed him aside with a big, slow hand. I was so astonished that my powers of speech left me. I had my mouth open to answer back, but no sound came. I think Mike was disappointed that we did not hotly deny his statement. Presently he began to go over his argument as if we were protesting over every point.

"You were away for two days. We know that you did not go to Golam Head, because there were no eels there. You did not go to the Aran Islands either. I asked one of the Hernons from Inishmaan, and he said you were not next nor near any of the three islands."

I found my voice to say, sourly:

"That Hernon sounds a very positive man."

"He was not so without reason," said Mike. "He was out fishing from his coracle two days ago and he saw the pookaun heading out for the Island of Horses. He was worrying about your safety, for he knows what happens to anyone who goes there. That's what brought him here to Inishrone today, to ask if you had come back yet. Myself and Andy were below in the boat, eating the old dinner, when he came sailing in. I knew by the looks of him that 'twasn't any of the usual things that brought him. When he told me, I advised him to go home peaceful-like, and not to be frightening your mothers. I said 'twould take a lot of Spanish ghosts to shake two clever young lads like yourselves."

Pat stirred a little. I guessed what was passing through his mind, that we should be grateful to Mike for preventing the silly Hernon man from alarming the whole island and maybe being the cause of a search party setting out in the boats for us. Mike sensed that our feelings toward him had softened a little.

"I like young lads to have their fun," he said largely. "If they are not venturesome when they are young, they don't grow up strong and manly. Isn't that right, Andy?"

He fetched Andy a dig in the ribs that made him bleat like a sick goat.

"But there is a difference between being a small bit venturesome and being foolhardy," Mike went on solemnly. "I've known the two of you this many a long year. I'd be no friend to you if I didn't give you this advice: never again to set foot on the Island of Horses."

"Why not?" Pat asked, in such an ordinary tone that it made Mike's warning sound silly.

"Ah, you may laugh. You may think it's all a joke. You may say it's an old wives' tale. But just think of the men you have known since you were small boys, fine men who went off, like yourselves, to the Island of Horses—Patcheen Moloney, and Jerry Sullivan, and Morty O'Neill—all fine men, and not one of them ever came back."

"But they were all drowned fishing," I protested. "They were caught in storms, far from home, the light of heaven to their souls."

"Amen," said Mike, and Andy bleated several amens in chorus until his father poked him into silence.

"The people didn't want to frighten you," Mike explained. "But you're old enough now to hear the truth." He lowered his voice. "Each of those men set off, like you, to the Island of Horses, just to see it. Each of them spent a night there, alone. Perhaps the reason why you were safe was that there were two of you. Not one of those lone men ever came back."

"What happened to them?" I asked eagerly, affected by the intense tone of his voice.

Mike grasped my arm and held it tightly.

"In the middle of the night the Spanish ghosts came riding up out of the sea. They were angry at finding a man on their island. They surrounded him, glaring, silently opening their empty mouths as they tried to speak. He screamed, but there was no one there to hear him. They lifted him onto one of the horses. They rode back into the sea with him, down, down, down into the sea, and so he was drowned."

My skin crawled, as I marveled at our escape. All around us on the island I had felt the presence of those malignant ghosts. Then, through my trance of horror, came Pat's cool voice:

"How do you know that story?"

Instantly, Mike was on his feet. We sprang upright too, for we felt his rage like a whirlwind sweep around us. He did not raise his voice.

"Very well, then. Go your own ways," he said grindingly. "Please yourselves and see where it will land you. Come along, Andy!"

And the two of them started off down the road toward Garavin. Andy giggled once and was silent.

We listened while their footsteps grew fainter. Then Pat said:

"I couldn't stand his old talk any more. Himself and his good advice! And did you hear him trying to make out that Spanish ghosts are worse than Irish ones, or Turkish ones? I saw those Spanish ghosts myself, and I thought they were peaceful, friendly little fellows!"

At this, my newly recovered confidence trickled away from me again. I dared not question Pat. There was something terribly convincing in his casually saying that they were little fellows. It was pitch-dark now, with neither moon nor stars. The beam of the lighthouse swinging across the sky and the lights from the cottage windows around us only made the night seem more full of strange, inexplicable shadows. Faintly the sound of the music floated down toward us. All at once, I noticed that the night air was cold.

"Yes, I'll tell my people that we found the colt wild on the Island of Horses," said Pat, as we started back toward the house. "And you can tell your father the same. It's clear enough to me now that the black horses are wild. Apart from their shoes, we should have seen at once that the other ones had harness marks on them, and that they had been clipped. But the blacks were wild, all right."

"How did the others get there?" I wondered.

"Mike Coffey could tell us that, I'd swear," said Pat. "It's certain sure that they did not swim. It's easy to see why he stopped the Hernon man from telling everyone where we had gone. Whatever he's up to, it seems that he does not want a fleet of Inishrone boats to set out for the Island of Horses."

Looking up toward the house, we saw the dim light of a candle against the blind of the room behind the kitchen fire.

"It looks as if the grandmother is gone to bed," Pat said, "but tomorrow, when the house is quiet, I'll ask her about the wild horses."

We had to be content with that. When we reached the house, John Conroy was singing the beautiful song called "Maureen de Barra." Never in my life did any song sound sweeter to me. I remember that I skipped into the kitchen out of the unfriendly darkness like a cat on hot bricks with seven ghosts clawing at my jersey.

6

WE HEAR THE GRANDMOTHER'S STORY AND SAIL TO ROSSMORE

I am always a great deal more sensible in the morning than at night. While we sat at breakfast next morning, I told my father and mother that we had been on the Island of Horses and that it was there we had got the colt. My father was cutting the top off his second egg, and I remember that his only sign of surprise was that he chopped it clean off in one blow, as if it had been a fish's head.

"I knew you were up to something," my mother said quietly. "Now that you're at it, you may as well tell us the whole story."

So I told them all about our landing on the island, and roofing the hut, and about the wild horses galloping past in the darkness. Then I told them about how we found the secret valley and how we had got the colt onto the boat and brought him home.

"Yes," said my father, "I was going to ask you today how you managed to get him up out of the sea into the boat."

He looked up at me quizzically from under his eyebrows. My mother said:

"Why didn't you tell us you were going there?"

"We were at sea for nearly an hour before we thought of it," I said.

"I bet Pat Conroy thought of it before you started," she said dryly.

"And up in Conroys' they're probably saying that only for Danny MacDonagh there would be no mischief," said my father. "Whichever of you started it, anyway, there's no harm done." He drew a great, long sighing breath. "And you roofed the hut, nice and comfortable, and baked your spuds in the hot ashes." He looked across at my mother. "I'll tell you something, ma'am. He's reared," he finished.

"Faith, then, he'll never go hungry," was her only comment.

I told them about the secret valley and how we had gone in and out of it when the tide was down.

"So the colt really belongs to Patcheen," said my father. " 'Twas his people were the last to live on the Island of Horses. That was a good island, if it was a bit wild in the wintertime, same. You can't have summer

all the year round. I could never rightly understand
how it got the bad name."

"Why didn't you tell us all this last evening?" my
mother wanted to know.

She was a very clever woman. She could see a hole
through a ladder better than anyone I ever knew. I said
to my father:

"I tried to get you away last night, but you wouldn't
come."

He looked a little uncomfortable at this, and my
mother said quickly:

"Why did you not tell us when you landed at the
quay?"

"We didn't want everyone going out to the island and
catching the horses," I said. "If you saw them there,
wild and free in their little valley, you'd say the same.
Pat said to ask you not to tell anyone about it."

"Is he telling his own people?" my father asked
sharply.

"Yes, but he's asking them not to tell anyone else
either."

"It will be hard to keep a secret like that," said my
father, shaking his head. "And the worst part of it is
that people will put legs under the story. The next
thing you'll be hearing is that there were fifty race
horses on the island, with fairy bridles on them, maybe,
to take you to the Land of Youth. My best advice to you
is to tell exactly what you saw and quickly. That way
you'll escape a lot of trouble."

"What trouble can there be? And sure, we needn't tell anyone today. Besides, the colt won't be here for long, because Pat is going to give him to John, for a present for old Stephen Costelloe."

Both my father and mother were overjoyed at this idea. Over and over again, my father said that the sight of the colt would stop Stephen Costelloe once and for all from talking about poor, penniless islanders. Anyone with an eye in his head could see that the colt was worth a mint of money, he said. He was so jubilant that he quite forgot his doubts about the wisdom of concealing the colt's origins. I need hardly say that I did not remind him. At this happy moment I asked if I might go over this morning to Rossmore with Pat and John and the colt, in the Conroys' hooker. They hurried me away at once, lest I be late. My father lamented bitterly that he could not come also. They both made me promise to observe every expression on old Stephen's face when he would first lay eyes on the colt, so that I could describe it all to them later.

Over at Conroys' I found that Pat had got the same reception. No one had doubted for an instant that the colt was wild and that it would be hard to dispute Pat's ownership of him, since Pat's ancestors had owned those of the colt. Then, the idea of giving the colt to old Stephen Costelloe had so delighted both John and his father that everything else had gone out of their heads. Pat's mother said she would prefer if John could keep the colt for himself, but she agreed that this would not be so effective as if the old man were to have him.

" 'Tis true," she said, "that old Stephen will be too busy thinking about the colt to remember Barbara."

Pat told me all this before we went into the kitchen. There was no one inside but the grandmother. She was sitting in her usual corner near the hob, and I was surprised to find that she looked rather subdued as she pulled at her clay pipe. She took it out of her mouth as we appeared and said quietly:

"Close out the half-door, boys, and come over here near me. Your mother is out feeding the pigs, and she'll be gone a while, I'm thinking."

We did as we were told. She made us pull up two creepie stools at her feet, so that we were all huddled together in the chimney corner. Still she looked anxiously toward the door before saying:

"Now, tell me. Is it really true that you found the colt on the Island of Horses?"

"Yes, really true," said Pat, "just as I told it."

"You found him down in the secret valley?" she persisted eagerly, while she watched us both closely.

"Why do you doubt our word now?" Pat asked, and he sounded a little impatient. "At first we said we found him swimming. Well, that was not true. But then we told the true story, that we found him on the Island of Horses."

"Don't be cross with me, agrá," she said.

She put out a hand like a claw and pulled at the sleeve of his jersey, as a small child does. Then I saw that there were tears in her eyes. Still she did not look sad, but rather triumphant, or victorious. She gathered herself together and sat up very straight. For one bright moment I saw a flash of her former beauty, now lost this many and many a year. We were both silenced by it. Then she went on:

"Often and often I told you about our life on the Island of Horses, and how we had to leave it at last when the men would not live there any more. It was too harsh and cold, they said. It was a bitter island. No living thing could endure it. But I knew different. They would not listen to me when I tried to argue with them. So one day we took everything out of the house down to the quay—kitchen tables, and dressers, and beds and linen chests. Oh, it was a sad, sad sight. Often I told you about it. The Inishrone men came with their boats, because ours were all broken up after that awful winter. We put the furniture in, and then the sheep and cattle and horses went in the bigger boats. When all the loading was done, our black stallion and mare were missing. The boats were so heavily loaded that they had to move out on the half-tide. If they had not, they would have had to wait for the next. The men were so anxious to be gone that they would not wait. They talked about coming back next day for the horses, but they never did."

"And where were the horses?" Pat asked, as she paused.

"I knew where they were." She gave a little cackling laugh. "I was the only one that knew. While everyone was busy with the furniture and the sheep and cattle, I got our black mare and the stallion, and I led them down into the secret valley, by a way that I know. You see, the men had taken them out of the valley at the low tide; the only way into the valley then was down over the cliffs. It took a long time. I was just back at the boats in time not to be left behind."

She paused again, and this time we had nothing to say. We were both thinking of that wild, determined girl, clambering down the mountain with the two horses. Presently she gave a long, satisfied sigh, and then she went on:

"I knew that it was not for nothing that our island was called the Island of Horses. I knew that our horses would not die. Often and often I wanted to go back there and see them. But sure, a woman can't do a thing like that alone. My own man, John Conroy, would have brought me, but in those days the people would have thought 'twas queer for a young married woman to go for a sail in a boat." She cocked an eye at us. "I used to find it hard enough to look sensible and quiet, like all the other women, with my heart and soul burning inside me for my own island. But that's all gone now. I'm eighty-one years of age now, and I can do what I like. I'm going to sail to the Island of Horses with you."

Pat's protests died away under her gaze. She was old enough to have sense, as she pointed out now, and she added that if anything happened to her it would be no great matter. At last she finished the argument by demanding:

"Do you think I'm going to go down into my grave

without ever seeing the Island of Horses again? If you won't take me, I'll take out the pookaun and go by myself!"

"There won't be any need to do that," said Pat soothingly, for she looked just then as if she would be quite capable of trying it.

She left us off then, to go down to the quay where John and his father would have the Conroys' hooker ready.

A few fields away from the house, the colt was grazing quietly. When we stopped at the gate and looked in at him, he came bounding over to us, his legs flying in all directions and his mane and tail streaming out on the wind. The old mare who was his companion in the field lifted her head slowly to watch his antics. Pat stroked the colt's neck and rubbed his forehead for a moment before opening the gate to lead him out on to the road.

"He's very tame," I said uncertainly, as I watched Pat slip the headstall over his ears.

"I know," said Pat. "I've been thinking of that all night. And look at the way he walked down the steps into the pookaun."

"Yes," I said. "And the way he came running over to you now."

"I was down to him early this morning with a bucket of milk," Pat explained. "But all the same, we'll never be certain sure about him until we find out how the other horses came to be on the Island of Horses."

He said the last part in a low, hurried way, as if he were ashamed to have any doubts after having listened to his grandmother's story. We walked along with the colt between us for a few minutes. Then he went on, with a little rush:

"I know he's mine. I feel it. And he knows it too. It hurts me all through my bones to have to give him away. But I suppose a Christian is more important than a horse," he finished disconsolately.

Then I said what had been in my mind since I had heard of the plan of giving this colt to Stephen Costelloe:

"There was a black filly in the valley too."

"I saw her," said Pat softly.

"We can make one more trip to the Island of Horses," I said. "We've promised to bring your grandmother, anyway."

"We have, so," said Pat.

From that moment it was as if a little lamp had been lit inside me, at the thought of going back to the Island of Horses again. It was plain that Pat was already transferring his affections from the colt to the filly that would so soon be his. For the first time, he gave a little jerk to the colt's headstall, almost as he might with any ordinary animal, and hurried him along a little faster.

Though the day was bright, the sky was scattered with huge, white, gray-edged clouds. As we came near the quay, the seagulls' cries filled the air, while they played with the high west wind. We could see that John and

Bartley Conroy had the mainsail of the hooker hauled
up, flapping against the mast, all ready to put to sea.
Even inside the harbor she was lifting uneasily.

Of course a little crowd of people had collected to
watch us go. The Dutch captain was there, sitting silently on a bollard, blinking in the sun like a good-
natured cat. Matt Faherty was there. He never missed
a spectacle of this kind. Derry Folan had hurried down
from the forge, leading the huge white horse that he had
no more than half-shod when he got word that something was happening at the quay. The owner of the
horse, Tim Corkery, had had to come along too, though
by the looks of him he would have preferred to have
gone back to his work. The strangest thing of all was
that the elder Miss Doyle from the post office had
actually left her little brass cage to come down to the
quay. She was little, and wizened, and stooped, and
she huddled herself into her towny coat as if she hated
the fresh air more than anything in the world. She and
her sister were foreigners from Galway, and the people
used to say that they fancied themselves as being a
little above the rest of us. They were always in bad
humor. More than once, I had thought that loneliness
was their trouble, but that they were too proud to show
it. Very few people visited them, because you had to
knock at their door and wait to be let in, instead of just
walking straight into the kitchen as you would in any
ordinary house. Still, the Dutch captain spent an evening there now and then, as he did in every house on

the island in turn. My mother sometimes went, too, and brought them fresh eggs and butter in the wintertime when those things were scarce. Perhaps this was why the elder Miss Doyle had risked being carried away by the wind, so as to see us embark.

As soon as he saw Miss Doyle, the Dutch captain stood up and gave her his seat on the bollard. She sat there like a queen while we solemnly paraded the colt for her. We got a discreet, cold nod for thanks.

"There's a storm blowing up," John called up to us cheerfully when we looked down into the hooker. "But I'd say 'twill hold off until the evening. Bring the laddo down now, and we'll be off."

Gently we walked the colt down the steps. He seemed not in the least put out at the prospect of another sail so soon. The watchers crowded to the edge of the quay wall to watch him step onto the foredeck and then skip lightly down onto the straw that had been laid for him below.

"He's the world's beauty!" Matt Faherty shouted above the wind. "Mind him well, now, let ye!"

"We will, faith!" Bartley Conroy called back.

A moment later we were sliding out through the mouth of the harbor. Looking back, I saw Matt still standing with his hands on his crooked knees, peering after us. It was only then that I noticed that Mike Coffey's hooker was gone from the quay.

Bartley wanted to haul in lobster pots at the end of the reef that forms the other side of the harbor. Remembering how the colt had resented my rockfish, I advised him to wait until the return journey. So we steered a course straight for the mainland.

Ours is a wild, rocky coast line. Everywhere, the long reefs that we call rosses point like fingers out of the sea. Where some land clings to these, there are farms and villages. The biggest of them is Rossmore, and right at the end of it was Stephen Costelloe's house.

It was a fine, big, two-storied house with a slate roof. The shop was a deep, cool room built onto one end of the house. There were trees all around to shelter it, but we could see the white walls gleaming through them as soon as we were half-way across from Inishrone. It was not a long sail, especially with a following sea and a strong west wind. The colt seemed to like it better today. Perhaps he preferred the bigger boat.

"From this out," said Pat, "he'll expect to be brought for a sail every day."

"He'd better get that notion out of his head," said Bartley. "We'll leave him at Corny O'Shea's until the wedding, and then we'll hand him over to Stephen. It's dry land for him from now on."

Corny O'Shea was a cousin of Bartley's who lived on Rossmore, not far from Stephen Costelloe's.

The wind drove us right in to the quay. One or two of the Rossmore men were loading their boats with turf, and they helped us to tie up to the quay. They did this silently, with hardly any talk, because at that time there was no love lost between the island men and the mainlanders. There was an old, old story behind this. But though the people's blood boiled whenever they thought of it, I always thought the real reason was that we had to buy our turf from the mainlanders, because there is no turf on the islands. Naturally enough, we hated seeing our good money going up the chimney in smoke.

As time went on, many other reasons for the feud grew out of the first one. We laughed at the turf-boat men for having no land. "Bádóirs" we called them, which simply means a boatman. But you should hear the way that an Inishrone man can say that simple word before you could realize its deadly insult. In return, the mainlanders' most villainous insult to us was in the two words: "Cosa bó," which means cows' feet. This referred to the wonderful shoes, made of rawhide with the hair on, that all the island men wear. If we tried to go about our daily business in leather boots, our island would be inhabited by lame men in a very short time. Our rawhide shoes are the only thing for the rocks, and they have the great advantage that they put no money into the shopkeepers' pockets.

So we gave the bádóirs no more than a single, curt word of thanks for their help and led the colt ashore. He caused as much of a sensation as if we had casually brought an elephant with us. It was only then, as we walked him up the quay, that I realized what a wonderful animal he was. The boatmen stared after him as if they had never seen his like in their lives. Neither John nor Bartley Conroy would look back, but I did.

There they were, grouped together with their mouths open and their faces full of an admiration and delight that they could not conceal.

Instead of pleasing me, the sight of them gave me my first feeling of real fear of the result of our trip to the Island of Horses. I turned back slowly and followed the Conroys up to Stephen Costelloe's house.

7

AT STEPHEN COSTELLOE'S HOUSE

The house stood a little back from the road, with a big sandy square in front of it. At the end where the shop was, several horses and carts were waiting for their owners. There were four saddled horses there, too, tethered to the hitching post, chatting to each other silently as horses do. These belonged to the mountainy men from the other end of Rossmore, who rarely troubled with carts if they could get on without them.

When they heard the colt approach, all the horses cocked their ears and moved a little forward to look at him. Then they whinnied very softly, as if they were too surprised even to make noise. Still, through the open door of the shop, we heard feet shuffle immediately.

We trotted the colt briskly around by the other end of
the building to the big yard at the back. It was an enclosed yard, paved with cobblestones, and with sheds
and cow houses all around. A few sleepy white hens
were pecking between the stones in the sheltered sunlight. At the far end, the back door of the kitchen
opened out into the yard, and it was by this way that we
entered the house.

Stephen Costelloe's kitchen was the finest I have ever
seen. It was as big as a barn, and it had an open fireplace wide enough to shelter a whole band of musicians.
It may have been designed for this very purpose, because it had a little stone bench built against its back
wall at either side of the fire. Unfortunately there was
hardly ever a dance held there, unless Stephen himself
had gone in to Galway to a fair, which did not happen
very often. Still, they said that a traveling man could
always be sure of a bed for the night there, but this
was probably Mrs. Costelloe's doing. She was as good-
humored as her husband was sour. Her daughter Barbara took after her, as all the world could see.

There was wonderful furniture in the kitchen. The
dresser was fronted with glass, to keep the dust off the
cups and plates inside. Its lower doors were made of
wood carved with every kind of thing that you find in
the sea—shells and seaweed and fish and down below a
little fat mermaid with a short tail, lying in a net. There
was a long, narrow, scrubbed table with carved legs
and feet like claws. The chairs all had arms, and there
was one huge padded one, covered with green leather,

that no one would dare to sit in except old Stephen himself.

He was not in it when we looked in through the doorway. John gave a little, quick sigh of relief when he saw that there was no one there except Barbara and her mother, and Kate Faherty, a woman from Inishrone who helped around the Costelloes' house.

As soon as she saw us, Kate slipped over at once and gently shut the door into the shop. I went over to the fire to talk to her, so that the Conroys could explain to Mrs. Costelloe and Barbara what had brought us. Barbara was a very fair-skinned girl, with light-brown, wavy hair. She had a friendly, comfortable look about her, and when you saw them together it was easy to tell that she would be like her mother when she would be older.

They all sat down at the table, and in a low voice John told them about the colt that he had outside as a present for Stephen. Mrs. Costelloe gave a little shriek of laughter at the idea of it. She stifled it immediately, and they all went out to look at the colt. A moment later Pat came back and opened the door into the shop. He stood there for a moment, looking around, and then he stepped inside. I had to force my eyes back to Kate, who was asking me all about the Inishrone people. She noticed that I was answering her absent-mindedly, but still she kept on with her questions as if to say that what was happening did not concern us. Even when Pat came back through the kitchen, half-running, followed by old Stephen himself, she kept her eyes on me. Out into the yard they went, but as they reached the back door, Kate and I got up without a word and followed them.

The scene was all that any of us could have wished for. There stood the colt, with Pat holding his headstall as if they were at a show, while Stephen walked around and around them. He was a small man, but square and stocky and broad-shouldered. It was no lie to say that I hardly knew him, for his usually mean little eyes were all lit up with a light that I had never seen in them before. Barbara and her mother stood back a little, together, watching him. John Conroy and his father were close by the door. Stephen put out a hand and touched the colt's neck. Then John turned suddenly and saw me. He went across and took the headstall out of Pat's hand, at the same time handing him a shilling.

"Into the shop with the two of you boys," he said, "and get some sweets. We'll be a while talking."

Stephen watched us benevolently as Pat joined me at the door. Just as we turned to go in, he said:

"Kate, tell Tom to give them a stick of peggy's-leg."

"Yes, sir," she whispered.

"I mean one between the two of them, of course," he called after her hastily, as she went inside.

Just before she led us into the shop, she stopped and winked at us.

"I didn't hear what he said last. Did you?"

"No," said Pat solemnly. "I did not, then."

At the other side of the door from the kitchen we found ourselves behind a high counter. In front of us there were bottles and jars of sweets. Kate reached up and took down a jar of peggy's-leg, opened it, and handed us a stick each. We slipped them quickly into our pockets, for the men who were drinking their porter at the far end of the counter had begun to laugh when they saw what Kate was doing. The little, red-haired, ferrety man who was filling their glasses came scuttling toward us.

"Kate Faherty, are you out of your mind? Do you want to land us all in jail?" he hissed angrily.

"Nonsense, my good man!" said Kate grandly. "Didn't himself tell me that they were to get a stick of peggy's-leg after the fine present they brought him from Inishrone."

"He said they were to get it?" The ferrety man looked at us with respect. Then, suddenly suspicious, he demanded: "What present?"

"A colteen not much bigger than a donkey, that looks to me like no horse I ever saw before. But sure, I'm only an ignorant old woman, and maybe he's no good after all."

By the time she had finished this speech every man had silently placed his glass on the counter and marched out of the shop. There were seven or eight of them, and we watched them file deliberately past the window on their way around to the yard to inspect the colt.

Left alone with ourselves and Kate, Tom, the ferrety man, ran up and down behind the counter twittering. He wanted to go out to look at the colt, and still he was afraid to leave the shop lest any customers might come in. Before he had made up his mind, the men were beginning to come back again.

"Well, boys?" said Kate impatiently to them. "What do you think of him?"

The nearest man was huge and dark-skinned and was wearing a bawneen jacket. He was a stranger to me. He shook his head sorrowfully as he answered:

"I'll never again sleep easy at night for thinking of that colt."

There was a low chorus of agreement from the rest. Kate lifted the flap of the counter so that we could pass through into the shop. I thought that Tom was rather pleased at this, as if he had disliked having us so near his precious jars of sweets.

"And to think of Stephen Costelloe owning that colt," the man in the bawneen was saying. "The very thought of it would make a dog bite his master."

"Sure, doesn't he own everything good in these parts?" said another man, whom they addressed as Colman.

Kate went back to the kitchen then, with the remark that she had a dinner to cook. We had moved over to sit on a bench by the door and were nibbling gently at the peggy's-leg. Now we found the eyes of all the men turned on us. They were quiet and speculative, but not unfriendly, except for those of Tom. He had a mean, calculating look about him, though I could not imagine what he could possibly have against us.

" 'Twas ye brought the colt, I'm thinking?" the man in the bawneen asked.

" 'Twas," said Pat.

"He's a fine animal," said Colman.

"He is, so," said Pat.

"Was he bred on the island?"

"He was."

"I never saw a colt like that out of the island before," said the big man.

"They're there, faith," said Pat.

There was silence for a while then. Through the door into the kitchen I could hear the murmur of voices. I guessed that the Conroys and the Costelloes were in there again, talking about the marriage. It was no wonder that Stephen, with all his wealth, was not pleased with it. Looking around the shop, anyone could see that he could buy and sell everyone on our island twice over. There was so much stock there that even in that huge room there was not space to store it all. The shelves and the counters were stacked with packets and tins of food and rolls of cloth for making dresses and suits of clothes. Barrels of porter were on the floor behind the counter, and open bags of bran and meal and oats leaned against the front of it. Hanging from the ceiling over our heads there were sides of bacon, and fishing-nets, and pieces of harness, and farm implements of various kinds, tied in bundles. There were coils of rope up there too, and a big bale of sailcloth hanging in a net.

The big man went on, after a while, as if he were talking to himself:

"When Stephen gets that colt for himself, I'm thinking

he'll like the island people a lot better than he does
now."

"Ah," said the others, and with one accord they
reached for their glasses and took a long drink.

Watching us closely, they could see that they had
rightly interpreted the reason why we had brought the
colt. At once they became more talkative and cheerful.
We were pleased not to be treated with suspicion any
longer, and gradually we relaxed from the stiff, hard
attitude that we had been taught to use to the Rossmore
men since our earliest childhood. All at once I began to
feel ashamed, for I could not remember a single thing
that I had ever done to make for friendship between us.
Indeed Pat and I had certainly added fire to the feud.
We nearly always pelted the Rossmore boys with stones
when they came in the turf boats with their fathers, and
we used to slip onto the boats when they were tied up
at our quay and turn the lobsters loose out of the pots
so that they would bite the boys' bare toes on their return. There and then I resolved never to indulge in
these amusements again. Like many a repentant sinner,
I thought that my life would be a great deal duller without my crimes.

Meanwhile the minds of the Rossmore men must have
been working in the same way, for now they began to
talk of the feud. They did not call it a feud, of course,
but a crossness and a coolness. It seems that after the
great rebellion of 1798 there was a priest called Father
Mannion on his keeping, as we say, in the neighborhood
of Rossmore. He used to stay a night or two in each

house, and the people counted it a great honor to have ancestors who had given him a bed. When the trail grew hot after him, he was to go to Inishrone, but right there on the quay at Rossmore the soldiers caught up with him, and that was the end of him. We have a beautiful ballad about him that would bring the tears from a stone.

A hundred and fifty years have gone by since that poor man drew his last breath. But if he knew the number of heads that were split and knives drawn since then in his name, I'd swear he would never lie easy in his grave. The trouble was that the Rossmore men accused the Inishrone men of sending word to the soldiers where they would find the priest, because they were afraid to have him on the island. On the other hand, the Inishrone men said that the Rossmore men had betrayed him, because they were jealous at seeing him leave them to go to the island.

Now, to our amazement, we heard the men say that it was likely enough no one betrayed him, but that the soldiers were catching up with him anyway. They said it was a terrible thing to see how bad blood could be made between neighbors on account of old stories that should have been long forgotten. Pat and I could not look at each other, lest we show our astonishment too openly and spoil everything. What I could not understand at first was why they should be so pleased that Stephen Costelloe was getting a present of the colt. They really had no love for Stephen. I could see that the same thing was puzzling Pat.

Then another customer came into the shop. She was a tall, thin woman with no teeth whatever. She did not seem in the least put out at this, but chattered away at top speed quite unconcerned. She had a basket of eggs under her shawl, and within ten seconds of her arrival she had Tom counting them out into the big box that stood on the counter.

"Three score and two, Sally," he said when he had finished, "but the two are duck eggs."

"And what's wrong with duck eggs, would you tell me? If you were reared on duck eggs yourself you mightn't be the little person that you are," said Sally briskly. "What are you giving me for them?"

"Six and twopence," said Tom, licking his pencil and calculating on his thumbnail.

"Little enough," said Sally resignedly, "but sure, 'tis no skin off my nose. Give me six and twopence worth of hen meal, Tom, boy. If they lay six and twopence worth of eggs they'll get the same in meal, and that's fair."

I knew there was a flaw in her reasoning somewhere, but I could not put my finger on it. While Tom was filling the meal bag for her, Sally turned her attention to the men.

"And what has ye all in here at this hour of the day?" she demanded. "Why aren't ye turf cutting this fine weather?"

"We were on our way to the bog," Colman explained, "and we dropped in here for a minute. The next thing was that these young lads and John Conroy and his dad came over from Inishrone with a present for Stephen

Costelloe—the finest colt that ever walked the soil of Ireland. You should see Stephen and he circling round and round the colt like a man that would be gone soft in the head, God between us and all harm."

"A present?" Sally looked at us sharply. "But he mustn't get it until after the wedding!"

Pat said, a little nervously:

"We're leaving the colt over in Corny O'Shea's until after the wedding."

"Good, good," said Sally. She brooded for a moment and then gave a short sour laugh. "That was the only way to get around him. Make a bargain with him. You'd think Barbara was a colt herself, instead of the finest girl in the three parishes."

The men murmured agreement. Now it was plain to be seen that it was on account of Barbara that they were all prepared to forget the long feud. I could see, too, that they were glad to see Stephen being bested at his own game.

Sally whirled around suddenly and said to Tom:

"And you needn't be noting down every word we say to pass it on to Stephen, because I'm going to tell him myself. Don't fear 'twill spoil the bargain," she said to Pat as he put out a protesting hand. "If Stephen has set his heart on that colt, nothing will put him off it, so we can say what we like."

She picked up her bag of meal by the neck, lifted the flap of the counter, and marched into the kitchen.

This was too much for myself and Pat. With a word to the men, we slipped outside.

"We'll go over to Corny O'Shea with the colt," said Pat. "We'd be a queer long time waiting for Stephen Costelloe to give us our dinner."

"Surely he would today," I said.

"Mrs. Costelloe would," said Pat, "but I wouldn't fancy sitting at the table with Stephen, knowing that he was watching every bite go into my mouth."

We went around to the yard. The colt was there, hitched to a ring in the house wall by a long leading-rein that must have belonged to the Costelloes. He was standing at the kitchen door looking in, listening to the conversation inside and twitching his ears with interest. The sunlight shone on his polished skin. Pat went over and undid the rein. The voices inside stopped.

"I'm taking this fellow over to Corny's," said Pat.

His father came to the door.

"Do, do. We'll be over after you."

A moment later Stephen Costelloe was at his side, with tightly folded lips, watching us lead the colt away. Behind his shoulder we could see Barbara and Mrs. Costelloe, smiling broadly and waving their fingertips to us. Just as we reached the gate, Stephen burst out:

"Be careful of him!"

Then he shut his mouth tightly again and half-turned away. But his eye showed clearly the terrible pain that burned in him when he saw the colt being led out of the yard.

When he had closed the wicket gate carefully, Pat said:

"It's working out fine, Danny. Oh, it's working better than I ever thought it would. Man, wouldn't it make a cat laugh to see the face of him!"

"Will he keep to his part of the bargain?" I wondered.

I did not know Stephen Costelloe at all well, for I did not often come to Rossmore. My father and I were usually too busy. But there were plenty of Conroys, and they had relations at Rossmore, so that they had both the time and the excuse to come whenever they felt like it.

"Oh, Stephen is a man of his word," said Pat. "Indeed I have an idea he thinks you can be as mean as you like so long as you stick to your bargain."

A quarter of a mile up the road was O'Shea's house. It was thatched and whitewashed, like our own, so that we both felt much more at home there than at Costelloe's. It was nearly one o'clock now, and a great smell of dinner came out over the half-door. When we looked in, Mrs. O'Shea was bending over the fire, lifting the lid of the huge pot of potatoes with the tongs. Her face was the color of her red petticoat, from the heat, when she turned around. She came waddling across with the tongs in her hand to let us in.

"Wisha, there you are, Patcheen," she said. "And Danny, too. Ye're heartily welcome. Pat, let you bring the little horse around to the yard. Corny has a bed ready for him." She gave a little cackle of laughter. "We heard all about him. Come in here, Danny, and tell me how did ye get on with Stephen."

So I went in and sat on the hob and told her how Stephen had fallen in love with the colt. Already the story had gone all through Rossmore, she said.

"And aren't ye the clever ones over there in Inishrone, to have colts like that to give away, and we not knowing a word about it?"

I made no answer to this, but again I wondered how long it would be before someone would discover that the colt had not been bred on Inishrone at all.

I lifted down the pot for her and carried it outside and strained the potatoes into a flat willow basket. She had a huge pot of golden-green cabbage, with a lump of bacon chuckling in the middle of it. I helped her to pile this on a dish, and then we pulled the table into the middle of the room. While I went out to call Corny and Pat, she laid knives and forks and salt cellars on the flowery oilcloth.

"What about Bartley and John?" said Corny when he came in at the door.

"They'll be here in a minute," she said serenely. "Don't you know they were both born at dinnertime?"

Sure enough, just as we sat down, Bartley and John came in. Corny was many years older than Bartley, but they were great friends. Since the last of Corny's sons had gone to America, Bartley had often helped him to mow hay or harvest the potatoes. Corny had very little land. There was no living on it for any of his sons, so he did not blame them for leaving him. But he was a sociable man, and I could see that he was pleased to be sitting at the head of a crowded table.

While we ate, they talked on and on about the colt. "The wedding is in six weeks' time, you say," said Corny. "There's plenty of young grass in the field for him that will last that length."

"Stephen said he would send you down a bag of oats," said John with a grin.

"Did he, now?" said Corny delightedly. "Faith, I think you have him this time. I never thought I'd see the day when Stephen would part with a bag of oats."

"He reckons that he owns the colt already," said Mrs. O'Shea. "Next thing he'll be wanting you to come and live in Rossmore and help him to run the shop."

"That's one thing that will never happen," said John.

8

WE SET SAIL IN A NOBBIE

Corny came down to the quay with us after dinner. In spite of the success of our expedition, we were all anxious to be at home again, where we need not watch our words and where everyone was friendly. Several of the Rossmore men were on the quay, too, and though they helped us to get the boat away with every sign of friendship, still it was all too new to be quite trustworthy, I thought. Corny himself was the only one of the men standing there waving to us who had never done us an injury, great or small. Apart from his being Bartley Conroy's cousin, he had never injured anyone so far as I knew. But the others had charged us too much for the turf, or had given us bad prices for our sheep and potatoes, or had fished in the places that were ours by ancient right. All these were small things, but taken together they showed clearly enough that to the Rossmore men we were foreigners. They did not feel that they owed us any of the special consideration that they kept for neighbors. Bartley remarked, looking back at the figures on the quay growing smaller as we pulled away from them:

"It will take time to get fond of them. They'll never believe us on the island when we get home and tell them what's after happening."

The wind and the sea were against us now, so that we made a slow passage homeward. The storm still held off, but we could see that it would break before night fell. Already we could feel that churning of the sea's floor that comes before a storm. The water was a dull, heavy blue, pitted on the surface by a pecking little wind. Every moment the slate-gray sky moved closer. I sat beside Pat in the bows, looking toward the Island of Horses.

"It's well not to be there now," I said, nodding toward it. "In a sea like this we'd never get away from it."

"We must go there for the filly when the weather settles," said Pat. He gazed longingly at the island so that it was clear he wished us there at this moment, no matter what the state of the tide and wind. After a pause he went on: "Weren't we the fools to think that all those horses could find food for the winter on a little island like that, with no one to plant an acre of oats for them or gather a rick of hay? It's a wonder that the blacks managed to get enough, year after year, to keep them going."

"Wild horses get along all right in America," I said. "Don't you remember Derry Folan's uncle from America saying about them, that they lived out winter and summer. He said they used to be a bit thin in the springtime, until the grass would come on."

"I remember," said Pat. "I suppose they have the caves to shelter in, out of the weather. Having to mind himself should make a horse very clever. You could tell by those other horses that they would never have the sense to come in out of the wet."

"But they were all good horses," I pointed out. "There wasn't one of them spavined or bony or knock-kneed. I suppose nothing but the best would be worth stealing."

Since I had realized that some of the horses had shoes, we had been aware that this was the only possible explanation of the presence of those horses on the island. We resented them all the more bitterly because such a mean solution brought our romantic vision of the island down to earth with a crushing force.

"We must get them off the Island of Horses somehow," said Pat with determination. "We could take them one by one in your pookaun, and land them on Golam Head, and let whoever brought them to the island have a fine search for them."

"We could take more than one at a time if we had this boat," said I. "The less ferrying we have to do, the better."

"But the two of us couldn't handle a hooker and mind

the horses at the same time." Pat looked doubtfully along
the length of the boat to where his father and his older
brother sat as deep in conversation as we were. He
leaned closer to me so that they could not hear. "Besides, we'll have the grandmother with us. I don't know
will she be a help or a hindrance."

"She might be able to keep the horses quiet while the
two of us sail the boat," I suggested.

"That's true, though it's my belief she'd only drive
them wild. But one thing is certain. If my father gets
wind of her plan to come with us, that will finish everything. He'll never let her go. And he won't want us to go
there alone, either, I'm thinking. If it wasn't for the
grandmother, I'd ask my father and John to come along
with us, and we'd clear off all the strange horses in one
day."

In the lee of Inishrone, the sea became calmer. Out at
the end of the reef, we hauled in our lobster pots, full of
indignant, crawling, black monsters.

Inside the little harbor, flurrying cats'-paws scurried
across the water. Long before we slid into our moorings,
a little crowd had begun to gather on the quay. They
could tell at once by our faces that our expedition had
been a success.

"Is the colteen safe?" Matt Faherty shouted.

"Safe and sound!" Bartley called back. "Eating his
fill at Corny's. We'll be dancing at the wedding in six
weeks' time."

It was clear that our success was regarded as a triumph for the whole island. The present of the colt was

not a bribe or a slavish effort to buy good will. What we all wanted was to show that we on the island could produce a spectacular dowry for our most valuable young man. All the better if the source of that dowry were something of a mystery.

"This is a great day, man, a great day!" said Matt.

We swung up the quay, all together. The men were in high good humor. The small children ran around the moving group excitedly, not understanding what it was all about, but feeling that something strange and wonderful had happened. The Dutch captain was one of the group. For all his huge bulk, he could move as fast as the thinnest man there. I have heard that bears have this same ability. As we passed the post office on our way to Matt's place, I glanced inside and saw the elder Miss Doyle safely back behind her brass bars again. She gave me a sour smile. I did not hold it against her, because it was a great trial for her to smile at all.

Two doors away from the post office was the public house. It was called The Suit of Sails, and it had a beautiful sign with a picture of a full-rigged ship swinging over the door. Matt kept the picture touched up so that it always looked new. It was the pride of Garavin village, and we did not like it when visitors to the island would look up at it and laugh, thinking that the name was funny. If Matt was perched on his old stepladder with a paint brush in his hand, as he so often was, he would climb down and deliver a solemn lecture on the words of the sign, until the visitors would blush and stammer and move away.

Matt's main reason for keeping his sign in such good trim was that it gave him an excuse to be out in the street watching what was going on. This same interest in the neighbors' doings left the inside of the shop in a state of the most impressive disorder. When there was no one in the shop, Matt could not bear to stay inside alone to clean it, and when he had customers, he could not bear to leave them for as much as a minute, lest he might miss a word of their conversation. Since he lived quite alone, the time when he was not in the shop was spent largely in cooking his scanty meals.

Once inside, Matt slipped behind the counter and began to fill glasses for everyone. Pat and I went down to the far end, where all the glasses that had ever been broken in the shop lay piled in a dusty heap. Matt brought us lemonade, and we sat there on two old barrels, sipping quietly and feeling suddenly very tired.

In a lull in the talk, the sign creaked loudly in the rising wind. I remember how just then, in the middle of our triumph, a black depression settled down on me. I could not understand it, though I have experienced the same thing before after a good day's fishing or at the end of a fine harvest. It was not the squalor of the dusty shop, for I was accustomed to that, and at that time I thought nothing of it. It was not that the events of the day had failed to reach the height of my hopes. Indeed I should have felt happier than I had ever done in my life before, surrounded by grateful, well-wishing neighbors. Instead I was filled with a great nervous fear and tension, which seemed to come from some fault or neg-

lect of my own. I glanced uneasily toward the door and
saw that the light had turned gray.

"What's the matter with you, Danny?" said Pat's voice
low in my ear. "You look as if someone had eaten your
candy!"

I tried to answer lightly.

"It's the storm, I suppose. And I'm a bit tired after
the day. I wonder could we slip out without being
noticed?"

"Nothing easier," said he. "Drink up and we'll be off."

I drained my lemonade and put the glass on the counter. No one so much as turned a head when we slipped
down off the barrels and went outside. I knew that my
father would soon be after us, for he was never a man
to stay too long from home. Bartley and John would be
with him, for they would be anxious to tell the news at
home, too. They would all have to stay for a while, of
course, so as not to show disrespect to Matt's hospitality.

"We'll go down to the quay and wait for them," said
Pat. "That's a dirty sky, and I'd like to be sure the boat
is safe."

It was not until we reached the top of the quay that
we saw the strange boat. It was moored to the quay
wall just behind Conroys' hooker. It was the kind of
boat that we call a nobbie, and very rarely seen in these
parts. It was considerably bigger than the hooker, dou-
ble-ended and rigged like a ketch with two masts. It
was not as handy a boat as a hooker, for all its extra
size, as we were soon to find out.

The strangest thing about it to our eyes was that instead of being tarred, it was painted dark blue. The only other painted boats that commonly visited Inishrone were the lifeboat and the Dutch captain's boat. Of course there were occasional yachts, but one would hardly call them boats at all.

We went straight down the quay to inspect the nobbie closer. Half-way there I stopped.

"Let's go home, Pat," I said suddenly. "Leave the old boat be."

"Is it not go near it at all?"

"I don't like it," I insisted, unable to say why.

"Wait you here for me, so," said Pat kindly, seeing that I was in earnest. "I won't be a moment. There's never a boat lands at Inishrone that I don't have a look at it, and this one is worth looking at, I'm thinking."

He said this persuasively, hoping that I would change my mind. But I would not stir. I sat on a bollard, turned my back on the nobbie, and faced away from the sea. This was why I saw what was happening up in the village.

A moment after I sat down, two men stepped out of the post office with the elder Miss Doyle. The younger Miss Doyle fluttered in the doorway behind them. The men were very tall and were wearing dark-blue overcoats, the color of their boat, and blue peaked caps. As they were strangers to me, I had no doubt that the strange boat belonged to them. Miss Doyle was obviously pointing us out to them, and while I watched they turned deliberately and began to walk down the quay toward us.

I was off the bollard like a stone from a catapult, and down the quay to Pat. He had boarded the boat, of course, and he was lying on the foredeck peering down into the little cabin when I reached him.

"Pat!" I hissed urgently. "Come ashore! The owners are here!"

"What harm?" said Pat carelessly. "Surely they won't mind if I have a look at their old boat."

From his position on the deck, he glanced curiously up the quay. Then, without a word, he climbed slowly ashore. I turned and stood beside him. Now for the first time I saw the strangers plain. Under their overcoats they were wearing the blue, silver-buttoned uniform of the Civic Guards.

There were no Civic Guards on Inishrone. We were a fairly law-abiding people and could provide little or no work for them. Now and then, the Guards from Rossmore paid us a visit, just to let us see that we were not forgotten. They were quiet, easy-going men always. The only sign of their trade was that they looked at you with the sharp eye of a good sheep dog. These strangers were altogether different. They seemed to be continually on the watch for criminals, especially the thinner one, who had a long, yellow, beak-like nose, for all the world like a herring gull. The other man was heavy-faced, with dead eyes like those of a deep-sea fish. It was he who spoke to us first, in a hard, suspicious tone and without a smile:

"Are you Conroy and MacDonagh?"

"We are," said Pat. "But it's likely you want to talk to our fathers. They're up there, in The Suit of Sails." And he made to go toward the village. The thin man barred the way.

"It's you two boys we want," he said. He made a great effort to seem friendly, but he could no more achieve it than his cousin the seagull could. "Come aboard the boat and we'll be talking."

We saw no harm in that. We did not know yet what had brought the Guards to Inishrone. It could be a question of wrack, for instance. When anything was washed up by the tide, we were supposed to report and hand it over to the Guards at once. We never did this, for wrack formed a necessary part of our living. I remembered a fine wooden door, with "Made in Sweden" stamped on it, that had floated in only last month and was now part of our cow house. I guessed that Pat's mind was running on the same kind of thing. Whatever it was, we thought it better not to wait until someone would come out of The Suit of Sails and see us and call the whole crowd out to listen to our conversation.

We stepped aboard the nobbie. The thin man said: "We have information about a stolen colt, that was brought here to Inishrone."

"He's not stolen," said Pat hotly, though he was almost breathless with surprise. "He belongs to me."

"That is not what the owner says."

"You know the owner?"

"He lodged a complaint. We traced the colt, with

some others, to the Island of Horses. We went to get boats to take them away, and when we came back this colt was missing. We failed to trace it until today, when we heard a story in Rossmore about the island men giving a present of a colt to a Mr. Costelloe. It is the same colt, without a doubt."

Though he paused, he did not seem to expect an answer. Pat stood as still as if he had died. The Guards' story had the awful stamp of truth about it. I thought how easy it would have been yesterday to have led the two men up to Conroys' field and to have handed them over the colt. But today the colt was a sign of friendship and a bond that could be broken only at the expense of greater enmity than ever before in history between the islanders and the Rossmore men.

At last Pat said:

"What have you come for?"

"You must come away with us, to Clifden," said the heavy man. "Perhaps we'll be able to arrange everything quietly. We'll show you the colt and you can tell us if he's the same that you brought from the island—"

"Have you got the colt?" For the first time Pat sounded defeated. "Did you take him from Corny O'Shea's place already?" He turned to me. "Oh, Danny, this is a sad day's work."

After that we had little more to say. We agreed between ourselves not to go up to The Suit of Sails and tell where we were going. The thin Guard said he would ask Miss Doyle to explain to our parents what had happened. We did not want to be there to see their

faces when they would be told that the colt was not
Pat's property after all. Pat said in a low voice to me:
"I wonder what will the grandmother say to this. Her
stallion and mare must have died on the Island of Horses
after all. I'm afraid she'll be sorely disappointed."

I did not know what to think. In spite of everything,
I could not yet believe that we had been so mistaken.
And still I told myself that the tale of an old woman,
over eighty years of age, was likely enough to be full of
queer fancies of her own.

The thin Guard went up to the post office and disappeared inside for no more than a minute. We helped
the other one to get up sail and cast off. He held on to
the quay wall with the boat hook while we waited for
his companion to return.

"It's going to be a dirty evening," said Pat, looking
up at the scuttling dark clouds.

The big Guard turned to glance carelessly at the reef
where woolly white waves were breaking heavily over
the rocks. He made no reply. Since he seemed so con-
fident, we did not press the point. I supposed that they
were as heedless of the weather as the lifeboat men,
because their business often took them out in storms
that would frighten an island man. I thought what wonderful seamen they must be, to be so brave.

There was still no movement at The Suit of Sails when
the thin Guard came back. On this day of all others,
Matt was finding the conversation inside so interesting
that he had not once peeped out to see that all was
well in the village. Now at the last moment I would

have given a great deal to have seen his long, eager head pop out through the doorway in the jerky, hen-like way that had so often made us laugh.

As soon as the thin Guard was aboard, the other shoved off with the boat hook. The wind swept over the sheltering wall of the quay and filled the mainsail. We rolled and lurched out into the middle of the harbor so suddenly that I almost lost my balance. Then the boat seemed to right herself, and we made for the harbor mouth steadily enough. A moment later we were out in the open sea.

9

SHIPWRECKED

From the very start I did not trust the nobbie. She had a way of going full tilt at the waves and burying her nose in them. Then she seemed to fall back on her heels while a terrible long shudder went through her. Though it was clear enough that she was in fear of her life, still she never learned from her mistakes. Once we got outside the reef, the seas pounded her timbers like sledge hammers. I looked back at the quay and thought it was already terribly far away.

All around us the waves rose up like hungry dragons. If the boat went down, I knew it would be quite fruitless to resist them. By the way in which Pat looked back toward the island and then at the waves, I could see that his mind was running on the same lines as my own.

The two Guards did not ask us to help them with the boat. They seemed to be accustomed to handling it together, but I thought they had a great deal too much sail up for safety. They showed no sign of fear, and I began to wonder whether it was that they were experts or that they knew so little about boats as to be unaware of the danger.

Half an hour out from Inishrone, I became convinced that the second possibility was the right one. If they had made for Rossmore, there would only have been a short distance during which we would have had no shelter at all, neither from Inishrone nor from the mainland. Since there was half a gale blowing now, an experienced sailor would have done this, changing all his plans accordingly, in order to save his skin.

But those bold heroes never even considered such a thing. They turned that boat into the teeth of the wild, Atlantic wind as coolly as if they were driving a horse and trap. Pat was not so patient as I was.

"What are you about?" he shouted above the horrid noise of the storm. "Do you want to send us all to Kingdom Come?"

The thin Guard's lips curled in a sour, superior smirk, but the heavy one answered:

"We're going to Clifden. We told you that."

"But the very worst part of the coast lies between here and Clifden," said Pat, hoarse from the effort to make himself heard. "We'll never make it."

"Those were our orders," said the heavy man with a

shrug. He did not bother to raise his voice, so that only some of the words reached us. "This is a strong boat. There's no need to be afraid."

Pat made no reply to this, since it was plainly useless to argue. He and I were sitting amidships, sheltered from the worst of the storm by the cabin. Still we were thrown about every moment by the lurching of the boat, so that already our bones were sore.

"It's only a mighty stupid person wouldn't be afraid of this," said Pat grimly to me. "Himself and his good strong boat! If you ask me, it's built like a hearse."

We were drenched with spray as the tops of the hurrying waves were flicked into the boat by the wind. The night was coming down in great black patches that moved nearer and nearer every moment. Soon they would cover us like a huge curtain. Off to the west, an angry sunset glowed. We were very hungry.

"Come along," said Pat into my ear. "If we don't get something to eat soon, we'll have no courage for whatever is before us."

We edged up along the boat to where the heavy Guard sat at the helm. He seemed more friendly than the other. We asked him whether there was any food on board and were greatly cheered to hear that there was a store of bread and hard-boiled eggs in the cabin. I offered to go and get the food, and for the first time the second man showed some signs of friendliness.

It was a dangerous task, and I knew I would have to be quick and careful. The only way into the little cabin was through a hatchway in the deck above. The bows of the boat plunged into every wave instead of riding over them as they would in any decent boat. Every time she plunged, the sea broke over her and washed along the cabin roof. This meant that I had to watch until she was climbing the wave, rush forward and lift the hatch, and get down below before she plunged again.

The thin Guard came forward to give me a boost up onto the cabin roof. I told him my plan, and he nodded approval, with what passed with him for a smile. A second after she plunged, I shouted:

"Now!"

I grasped the cabin roof and swung upward, assisted by a mighty heave from the thin man. But he held on to my foot, as if he were afraid to let me go. I kicked at him frantically.

"Hands off! Let go, you fool, let go!"

He let go. I darted forward to the hatch, but the time lost while the thin man had held on to my foot was almost the cause of my death. The bows were plunging into the next wave. The wind howled in my ears. I felt the sea wash over me, almost gently, while I clung to the hatch. My fingers slipped a little, so that I thought I was lost. Even in that moment I knew that if I went overboard, they would never succeed in picking me up. The nobbie would be a hundred yards away before they would be able to start turning. I thought it a miserable end.

Then I noticed, after an age, that her nose was climbing again. With one gasping breath, I skipped down through the hatchway like a cat stealing a fish. I stood on the ladder and looked back toward the stern. Pat's face was white in the ugly gray light. The eyes of the other two were fixed on me, so that I read in them the reality of the danger I had just passed. It was as plain as a pikestaff that all three of them had fully expected to see me washed off the cabin roof and down into the black depths of the sea before their eyes. The difference between them was that whereas Pat looked horror-stricken and sick with fear for my safety, the other two looked disappointed.

Silently I descended the ladder, letting the hatch fall into place after me. Now for the first time I saw that there were two portholes in the bows, giving a dim light. This was another strange thing. I had never before seen portholes in a nobbie. Usually the only light came into the cabin through the open hatchway. I looked at the portholes for a long time, in a kind of dream. Over and over I said to myself:

"Very strange, very strange."

The words meant nothing to me, for my head was empty of feeling. I shivered suddenly and burst into tears. Even while I sat down on an old sack and gave away to my terror, I was able to feel pleased that Pat was not there to see me. Gradually I recovered the use of my wits enough to feel foolish. I was a little consoled when I remembered how Tom Kenny, a hardy man of middle years, had cried like a baby for five minutes after he had almost been crushed by a falling mast at Rossmore.

I opened the one locker that the cabin contained

and found the food. Then, before starting back to the others with it, I paused to think of the extraordinary impression I had got when I looked back at the two men from the safety of the hatchway. They had looked disappointed, I had thought. If I were right, this could only mean that they had hoped I would be washed overboard. The idea was fantastic, until I remembered how the thin man had held on to me until it was almost too late. Thinking of this now, it was easy enough to see that he had done it deliberately. That man was not excitable or given to sudden panic, I felt sure.

I knew that there is a kind of person who derives a special pleasure from the misfortunes of others, without going so far as to wish them ill or to injure them. Such people will always be found talking over the sins of a poor criminal, pitying his wife and children with righteous satisfaction, and prophesying his further downfall. They are the same people who gather closely around the victim of an accident, hungry for the sight of him to glory in afterward. It occurred to me now that Guards must be hardened to misfortune and that without it they would be lost for something to talk about.

But try as I would, there was no getting over the fact that the Guard had held on to my foot until I was in the worst possible danger. He was a fine protector of the people, to be sure!

Then, all at once, I realized the truth. It startled me so much that I let go my hold on the locker door and was sent spinning across the cabin floor among the ropes and tins that lay in a heap in the bows. All around me the sea thundered, and the boat rose and plunged and shuddered. But I just sat there, like a blind man who suddenly sees, and who is so overjoyed that he does not care if the first thing that meets his eyes is a charging bull. Now I knew that they were not Guards at all.

I went back over every moment of our time with them. One after another, I remembered the things that had seemed wrong about them. Their unfriendliness had been the first and the most surprising thing. Then there was the fact that they had not gone up to The Suit of Sails and spoken to my father and Pat's. I realized now that no Guard would take away two boys unless their parents came, too. Another point was that the real Guards would not have come in a clumsy, unmanageable sailing boat in a storm like this one. They always came in the lifeboat, which had a powerful engine and could have weathered a much worse storm with ease. Besides, they would have known that we could not leave the island and that they could afford to wait. The longer I thought about it, the more I realized that their only resemblance to Guards was in their height and in their clothes.

And if they were not Guards, who and what were they? They had known our names, and they had mentioned the Island of Horses. It did not take any great intelligence to see that they had something to do with the presence of those other horses on the island. The only other person who seemed to know something about the Island of Horses was Mike Coffey. And Mike's boat

had already left the quay when we had set out for Rossmore this morning.

I wished I could consult with Pat as to what we were
to do next. Still, it was plain enough to me that there
was nothing to be done except to stay alive until we
could get ashore. That was not going to be easy. Even
if the two men did not succeed in throwing us overboard one at a time, it was doubtful whether the boat
would weather the storm much longer. Then we would
all go down together, innocents and scoundrels alike,
and the fish who would nibble our bones would not be
at all particular as to which kind they would begin on.

This thought made me spring upright. Whatever were
my chances of escape, they would disappear completely
if I were below when the boat foundered. It occurred
to me now, too, that Pat might come looking for me,
since I was so long gone. He might fall an easier victim
to the thin man's treachery than I had.

The bread and the eggs were stored in an old linen
bag. I swung it by the neck, and climbed up the rickety
companion ladder. Just as I lifted the hatch I had a
moment of horror. What if I found Pat gone without a
trace, and the two men grinning and licking their chops
like a couple of hungry cats on the prowl? I knew that
they would only have to set upon me together and heave
me overboard and that there was little I could do to
save myself.

To this day I do not know why they held back. Often
I have thought about it, and I can only conclude that
they had some remains of conscience which made it

difficult for them to be as callous as they would have liked. To ease their own minds, they would have had to make our deaths look like an unfortunate accident.

When I poked my head up through the hatchway, I was mighty relieved to see Pat standing beside the heavy man at the helm. The storm had increased still more, and the sea was racing in dull, gray, sloping sheets, smooth and terrible, like steel. The boat's timbers creaked and moaned as if she were being crushed to matchwood under a giant rock. While she rose and fell on the monstrous waves, her masts swayed and bent under their weight of sail. As far as I could see, every ounce of canvas was still up. In despair I saw that it was a miracle she had lasted so long.

I could hardly see the coast line, for the black night had moved closer. On the desert of water around us not a sail showed but our own. Anyone looking out to sea and watching our mad race would surely think that everyone on the nobbie must have been washed overboard and that she was rushing, wild and free, to her ruin.

I watched my chance to climb out on to the cabin roof and drop quickly down to the deck below. The wind tore and clawed at me as I worked my way astern. As I came closer I saw that Pat's face was full of rage and despair. He was shouting into his companion's ear:

"For pity's sake, will you have some sign of sense and lower that sail! I'm sick and tired of telling you that you'll sink your old boat. She'd be no loss, but that we'll all go with her."

The heavy man, looking not at all impressed, said: "We're in a hurry to Clifden. She's going fine."

Pat turned to me.

"Danny, will you try to explain to this booby that he's not driving a donkey cart. What will be the end of us all?"

"I'd give her another ten minutes of life," said I. "She's the worst boat I ever set foot in, without a word of a lie, and even a good one couldn't last long in a storm like this."

If we wanted to frighten him, we certainly got our wish. Even in the fading light, I saw his face turn green. Until now he had handled the helm with some little skill, though he was no expert. Now he gave it a sudden jerk to leeward. She heeled over, and her gunwale went under. When she righted herself, it was in a heavy, sluggish way, for she had taken a few barrels of water aboard. I felt it wash about my bare toes. The thin man came plunging toward us.

"What are you doing? Do you want to finish us?" he snarled.

"The boys say we're finished anyway," the heavy man stuttered, while he shook with panic. He took his hands off the helm and held his head between them, wailing: "I wish I was at home, so I do! I wish I had never come out in this—"

Again she lurched and heeled over. This time she righted herself more slowly. We were ankle-deep in water. The mainsail flapped as the boom swung across. She settled a little by the stern.

"She's finished, Danny," said Pat's voice in my ear. "She won't last your ten minutes, I'm thinking."

The thin man was lowering the mainsail, letting it fall in a great heap to add to the confusion. The heavy man was saying his prayers. I guessed it was high time for him. I realized that I was still holding the linen bag of food, well splashed now with sea water. Beside me, Pat was working feverishly at a water barrel, emptying it out and then hammering the bung securely home, with a stone from the ballast. Then he got a length of rope and looped it around the barrel twice.

"That's all we can do for a lifebuoy," he said into my ear. "We're not done for yet." He raised his voice to call out to the two men:

"You'd better get out of those big boots and those heavy clothes, or they'll sink you!"

At once they began to do so, the heavy man in a twittering flurry that made his task twice as hard, and the other with a slow and impressive deliberation. I noticed that both of them worked clumsily, as if the clothes were strange to them.

They were still at it when, with a short, sharp crack the mainmast broke in two. It fell among us and lay alongside the tiller as if it were tired.

"If that had happened when the mainsail was up, we'd have been over," said Pat. "And if this were any decent class of a boat at all, she'd lie to right here, sweet and comfortable. But look at her! She's like a whale!"

Indeed she was behaving now as I have heard a dying whale does, banging and thrashing about in the sea in a way that I never before saw a boat do. We bailed, but we could not bail the Atlantic Ocean dry, and that would have been the only way to save that nobbie. The two men were useless. The heavy one prayed and blubbered still and said he was a martyr to colds, which made me smile even in the midst of our misfortune. The thin man spent his time in cutting free the splintered end of the mast with his pocket knife and in clearing it of its various ropes so that he would have something to which he could cling. When the other saw what he was doing, he gave a wild cry, like a sea gull's, and plunged forward to grasp the mast. He held it as if he were already drowning. The thin man sneered, but he let him hold on.

We were very cold, standing in water over our knees.

"Maybe I'm daft," said Pat, "but I'm going to eat a bit out of that bag you have there. If it does us no good, it will do no harm."

Dragging our barrel with us, we moved forward inch by inch and braced our backs against the cabin. The bows of the boat were higher out of the water than the stern, and here we had a little shelter from the wind. It was extraordinary how this small relief pleased us. We waved to the men, and they came forward, too, dragging their mast with them. The thin man turned a covetous eye on our barrel, I thought, but he said nothing.

With the last of the daylight, we got the food out of the bag. We dared not use both hands, so we plunged at random and ate whatever we hauled up. It was soda-bread, damp and salty now, but delicious to our starved palates. There were hard-boiled eggs, too, as the heavy man had said. They were in their shells, and we chewed shells and all as if they were the best of good food. There were two for each of us and many thick slices of bread. We ate until the bag was empty of everything except a few sodden crumbs. Then, with nothing more to occupy us, we waited for the boat to sink.

10

WE COME ASHORE AND
MEET LUKE THE CATS

I had never been shipwrecked before, and I was quite surprised at how long it took for that nobbie to go down. The cabin seemed to act as a kind of bulkhead, keeping her bows above water. We dared not look into it, but it must have been bone dry inside for a long time. The ballast had shifted to the stern, of course, and washed about there most miserably. Presently her bows were almost pointing to the sky, and we were hanging on by our hands to the cabin.

By a great mercy, it was not pitch dark. A full moon looked out from among the ragged, flying clouds, and even when it was covered, there was a kind of brightness about us. The huge, hungry waves, which had been so ugly in the dull daylight, were beautiful now in the soft light of the moon. The storm had slackened a very little with the fall of night, and we were glad no longer to be deafened with the shrieking of the wind and the sea. Pat spoke close into my ear:

"She's drifting nearer to the shore every minute. If it wasn't for that, I'd say we should leave her now. As long as she lasts, she'll serve us better than the old barrel."

I said:

"Pat, are you not afraid?"

He did not answer for a moment. Then he said:

"I am, but I don't see the sense in it. 'Tis better not to think of that. I'd like to be at home now, so I would."

"Do you think the wind is less?" I asked, just for the sake of talking.

"That storm is nearly blown out," said Pat.

"Then perhaps the boat won't sink after all?"

Even as I said it, I knew that there was no hope. Pat gave a little snorting laugh.

"She's walking on the ocean floor this minute, I'd say," he said.

She was indeed like a swimmer who has got out of his depth and, having turned back toward the shore, cautiously feels downward first with one toe and then with another, hoping to find the bottom. I did not feel in the least sorry for her.

When she did go down at last, it was softly and gently, like a basking shark. We knew it was going to happen, for we had felt the bows settle gradually. The water had found a way in at last and was filling the cabin. We had harnessed ourselves to our barrel long since, but loosely, so that we could get free if it began to sink. Silently the two men had watched us and had followed suit with their piece of mast. But they could not bring themselves to hang on as long as we did. A good ten minutes before the nobbie went down they had launched the mast as if it were a boat and had gone tossing away on the gilded, dark waves. Inside a minute we had lost sight of them.

"God give them strength to hold on," said Pat after a moment.

We did not mention them again nor peer after them.

Presently the whole of the boat was submerged. Still we stood on the cabin roof, held upright by the barrel which turned out to be a splendid lifebuoy. It was bitingly cold. The waves slapped our faces, and I remember that this offended me. I felt no panic now, and I think it was because I had exhausted that sensation when I had almost been washed off the cabin roof.

Then, all at once, we were swimming. The last little pocket of air had filled with water, and the nobbie was gone down for good and all.

"There's one bad boat less in the world," said Pat grimly.

After that there was no more talk. Every ounce of breath was needed for the business of keeping alive. We held the cross-rope of the barrel short, but still we had to swim a stroke with the free arm to keep afloat. Now that we were so low in the water, I knew that we might toss about in the same spot until Doomsday or until we would become exhausted and let go, perhaps to sink down into the nobbie where she lay on the sea's floor. Dead or alive, I did not want to see that boat again.

It was well for us that there was a strong tide running. Within a few minutes we began to notice that we were drifting slowly. For all we knew, we were traveling to America. Down among the waves, we could see no sign of land, though we knew that we were not far offshore. It was bright moonlight still, so that we could see each other, and this was a great comfort to us in our desolation.

It was a strange thing that while we had to fight the waves we had no time to despair. But as the wind dropped and the waves became slow, curving rollers, a terrible languor and heaviness took possession of me. My arm, stretched out to hold on to the barrel, looked as long as an oar and ached with an ancient pain that seemed to have had no beginning. A little voice inside me said that it would be better to let go. My arm said the same: "Let go. Let go. You're hurting me." Down into the soft, rocking sea I would go, to sleep, to sleep, to sleep.

I let go, and for one delicious moment felt the pain in my arm diminish. But when my head ducked under the water, I woke up quickly enough. The rope around my shoulders still held me to the barrel, and I was very glad to reach out and haul myself, spluttering, head and shoulders out of the water. But in that moment when I had gone under, I had felt sand under my feet.

Still it was an age before we got ashore. Though the storm was almost over, the waves were thundering on the sandy beach in a boiling white welter of foam. Each time we found the bottom we were dragged back again, away and away out to sea, to float helplessly until the next wave would go racing in with us. We hit our heads together and against the barrel. We were turned over and over like clowns at a circus. We swallowed salty mouthfuls of the bitter sea. We had gone in and out many, many times before we realized that it was the barrel, which had served us so well until now, that was hindering our landing.

The next time that we were dragged out, we slipped out of the ropes that had harnessed us to the barrel and held on with our hands only. There was a moment or two in which we hung there, and then we felt the long drag again as the next wave carried us toward the shore. Right in the midst of the crashing breakers, we let go. I remember that I lay like a stone, face downward in the shallow water, suddenly helpless without the barrel. All around me was white, thundering water, beating me down into the sand. Then, as I heaved myself upright, the wave trickled away, and I was left high and dry. With my last remaining wits, I forced myself to move out of reach of the ravening sea. I went on my knees, slowly and painfully, like a medieval pilgrim. When I came to soft sand, I lay down at full length.

Still I knew I should not rest, that there was something still to be done. Hardly knowing why I did it, I raised my head a little to look down toward the sea.

Then I saw Pat, crawling slowly toward me; I waited until he lay beside me, and a deep peace filled me, such as I have never experienced since. I felt his hand reach out to touch me, and in that instant I fell asleep.

It was the sun that woke me, and the quietness. After the thundering noise of my dreams, this seemed very strange and unnatural. The waves washed in onto the sunny sand with a gentle, whispering sound that fell away into silence for a moment before starting again. When I lifted my head, I could see that there was a huge smooth strand below me, with a few weed-covered rocks at the water's edge. Down there I could see Pat, stooping low over the rocks. All around me was a great ring of grass-covered sand hills. The sand was almost as white as lime, and it looked delightfully clean and ordinary after our night of horror.

I stood up painfully and slowly, for my bones were sore. However, I found that with each step that I took toward Pat I felt a little better. When I came near him, I saw that he was laughing at me. It was no wonder, for I was walking like some huge water bird that is ungainly on dry land. My joints were as stiff as if I were ninety. I have never since laughed at the old men who hobble down to Inishrone quay to sit in the sun, holding themselves upright with one hand gripping at their coattails.

Pat told me that he had been awake for half an hour. "I was as bad as yourself at first," he said. "You'll be fine in a while. Oh, man, isn't it grand to be alive!"

He had the front of his shirt full of shellfish, but we

could not bring ourselves to eat them, they looked so cold and tough. He let them fall back into the rock pool in which he had gathered them, and they bubbled happily.

The sea was like pale, gray-blue satin, with a long, smoother line far out where the current was. There was one boat out there. It looked like a bird, because we could not see where the sea joined the sky. It was about eight o'clock, judging by the height of the sun.

Our clothes had half-dried, but they were heavy and sticky to our backs. Now we began to talk of a house where there would be a fire, and soda-bread, and butter-milk, and clean, dry clothes, and someone to send a message to Inishrone to say that we were safe.

"Likely enough they'll think we're drowned when the Guards in Clifden report that we didn't arrive there," said Pat.

Though our hearts were heavy at the thought of the fate of the two men, this was the first time that either of us had mentioned them. Only now did I tell Pat of my conclusion that they were not Guards at all, but confederates of Mike Coffey. Pat stood stockstill. We had reached the grassy edge of the strand. He turned to look down at the sea, and then he said savagely:

"Do you mean to tell me that we could have spent last night at home in bed? That we needn't have come out with those two rascals at all? That we needn't have nearly lost our lives out there in the storm?"

"That's my belief," said I. "I only thought of it when

I went down to the cabin to get the food, and I got no chance to tell you since."

"And I told them that Mike Coffey was up to no good," said Pat, shaking his head in wonder at himself. "I told them that while you were below. I said I was sure he knew something about the horses, and that they should watch him. They said, thanks very much, they had never thought of Mike, and he was very free to go and come with his boat, and that I was a fine, observing sort of a boy. And they must have been laughing up their sleeves all the time. I hope—no, that's a death I'd wish to no man. If they're alive, they've got a fright that will keep them quiet for a while."

As we continued on our way, I told him how the thin man had held on so long that I nearly went overboard. Even now, after all that had happened since, I remembered that little moment with a thrill of horror.

At the top of the strand a huge expanse of sand hills, covered with short grass, stretched away before us. As we made our way across it, everywhere we came upon rabbits' villages. These were all the same, a dozen or so of little round doorways and a pattern of roads going in and out. There were fresh tracks of little feet, and once there was a scurry of flying sand as we approached, but we saw no sign of twitching ears or small white tail flashing into a burrow. It was queer to think of all those little panting bodies cowering under the earth, waiting to come out again when we would have passed by.

It seemed an age before we topped the last little sand hill and saw a road before us. We were weak from hunger as well as from last night's ordeal, and we had to sit down for a few minutes before covering the last part of the way. Down there, at the edge of the road, was a tiny white house. I can still see it as I saw it then, set with its gable to the road, in a wild rocky field as carefully walled in as if it were a paddock fit for a race horse.

"There's smoke," said Pat after a moment. "Someone is inside."

Sure enough, a wisp of smoke no bigger than would come from a pipe trickled out of the chimney. A mile or more away to the east we could see other, bigger houses. All around the little house were acres of rock and fern and heather. Near it there was a potato patch, freshly dug. A single black cow foraged in the one good field that we could see.

Presently we heaved ourselves upright and started downhill. We found a little boreen, heavy with cold white sand, leading up from the shore. After a while its surface changed to soft mud and grass, and then it led us straight to the little house. Soon we were standing in the grassy open space before the door, staring in.

The half-door was shut. Then, while we watched, a man appeared and leaned his elbows comfortably on the top of the door. He was tough and hard and wiry, like a thorn tree. His face and his hand, curled around the bowl of an old clay pipe, were the color of a smoked herring. His little eyes blinked at us through steel-rimmed spectacles that added to his air of ancient wisdom. He examined us shrewdly, from our damp clothes to our salt-spiked hair. When he spoke, his voice was soft and a little hoarse, as if from lack of use.

"You've been in the sea," he said. "Your boat is gone, I'm thinking, after the storm."

We nodded. He leaned more comfortably on the door and brought up his other hand to cradle his pipe.

"That just proves what I'm always saying." He sighed with a mixed air of impatience and satisfaction. "There should be a factory here for canning fish. Now, if there was a factory, you wouldn't bother going out fishing on a stormy night in a bad boat. You'd be working in the factory, drawing your money every week like a lord, instead of being in daily danger to life and limb out on the wild ocean. That's what I told the Department. Two hundred and forty-seven letters they've had from me in the Department about that canning factory—and not a stamp on a single one of them!"

His eyes sparkled with triumph. Pat said, a little tremulously:

"Please, sir, we're hungry."

"You see!" said he. "If you were working in my factory, you wouldn't be hungry. Why? Because you'd be a wealthy man. Because you'd have money in your pocket—"

"But who would catch the fish?"

I could not resist asking the question, in spite of my

exasperation. A moment later I wished I had kept silent. He turned a coldly contemptuous eye on me, glinting angrily through his glasses.

"It's people like you that are ruining this country," said he. "People without vision, without enterprise, without imagination. People with small, mean minds. People that are only out for themselves." He laughed delicately. "Of course, you must be from one of the islands. I hear they're very backward out there."

"Backward they may be," I said hotly, "but they would never leave a person standing hungry on the doorstep. They would ask him to come in and sit by the fire. They'd ask him had he a mouth on him. They'd help him on his way, instead of blowing old talk at them about factories for making fishes out of the little stones and selling them to the fairies!"

"Easy on, Danny," said Pat quietly.

The man was sorely offended, but he was opening his door to us at last.

"Come in, then," he said stiffly. "You are in the right, of course. I should have asked you to come in at first. I haven't much to offer you, but what I have is yours."

Now I felt ashamed of myself, though he had surely been as uncivil as I had. Still, something in the words he used or in the dignified way in which he stood aside to let us pass into the kitchen made me realize that he was a little different from most of the people of those parts. Perhaps the long shelf of torn books beside the fireplace was the explanation, for he spoke like an educated man.

Though the fire was small, it was very bright. We sat on either hob, and our host knelt between us to put on more turf. Soon our clothes were steaming and our shins glowing with the heat. As my body warmed slowly, I felt the terrible fear of last night's experience lift from me. I wrapped my arms around my knees, happy to be safe on dry land. Until that moment I think I had almost expected a long, cold arm to reach out and twitch the two of us back into the salt sea again.

I began to look with interest around the little house. It consisted of a single room, if you did not count the open loft that covered half of the kitchen. There were a great many cats up there, lifting their heads one by one to look down into the kitchen. As the fire grew bigger, they began to climb cautiously down the rickety ladder in the corner. At the foot of the ladder, each one stretched its hind legs once, yawned, and then padded silently across to the fire. They sat in a row, stealing sidelong glances at us from time to time in that slinky way that cats have. As soon as the big ones were all settled on the hearth, an army of little ones began to assemble behind them. They were all sizes, from staggering, fortnight-old kittens to narrow-shouldered, long-tailed highway-robbers of six months. They crawled out from behind cupboards and sacks and down off the old iron bed in the corner. Some of them, as we now saw, had even been roosting on the dresser among the cups and plates.

"I like cats," said our host. "I'd never be able to use up the milk of the cow without them."

"You're well enough supplied with them, sir," said Pat.

"I am that. What I like best about them is that they let me do the talking."

I dared not catch Pat's eye, for I was afraid that we might give offense by laughing.

"They call me Luke the Cats," our host went on. " 'Tis an honorable name. I'd rather be called Luke the Rats, or even Luke the Cockroaches, than plain Luke Faherty as I'll be named on my coffin. To be distinguished for something—that is the thing."

It was on the tip of my tongue to suggest that he might yet be called Luke the Fish Factory, but I restrained the impulse.

He got out an evil-looking dish of cold boiled potatoes and spilled some gurgling sour milk out of the churn into two chipped mugs. A great splash of the milk streaked the floor. Some of the cats sloped across to lap it furtively.

Presently Luke pulled three stools over to the grimy table on which he had laid out this unsavory meal and said:

"Let you come over now and eat your fill. You'll excuse me if I don't eat with you. I have but the two mugs."

There was nothing for it but to move over to the table and begin to eat. Luke sat at the table, too, from politeness, and watched us anxiously for signs that we were enjoying our meal. He lent us his pocket knife to peel the potatoes. He urged us to dip the pieces in the sour

milk, which he said would give them a savor as good as
any salt.

"Potatoes and sour milk—that's what I live on," he
said. "And I'm as healthy as a fish on it!"

And he started off on a long discourse on the evils of
eating good food. He said it makes people soft and helpless. He said that in his grandfather's time the men grew
a good twelve inches taller than they do now and that
they could spend three days out in the fishing boats without sleep. The annoyance he aroused in us took our
minds off the nastiness of what we were eating, and this
was a good thing. We managed to swallow several potatoes each and by closing our eyes to send the sour
milk after them.

Back at the fire, I found that the food had put life in
me again. I noticed that there was a sparkle in Pat's
eye, and a moment later he leaned across the fire toward
me to whisper:

"In the olden times, Danny, I bet the big fellows used
to eat the little fellows to make a good diet with the
potatoes and milk!"

I gave a little shriek of laughter. Luke turned around
from his task of clearing the table and then I had to
pretend that one of the cats had bitten me. He looked
at me fixedly for a moment, but he was too polite to
express what was clearly in his mind, that I had been
teasing his cats. I was saved by the fact that the biggest cat chose that moment to spring onto my knees and
settle down in a crouching, purring heap. I stroked his

head gratefully. Luke's face lost its suspicious look, and he turned back to the table.

We were silent until he had finished putting the remains of our meal into a wooden tub.

"It's for the Widow Joyce," he explained, "a decent poor soul with three pigs. I'd scruple to waste the good food. I thought of keeping a pig myself, but I couldn't stand them. They're mean, sly creatures, all stomach and lies. A pig would mislead his own mother, so he would."

He said this in such a hard, bitter tone that I would have liked to ask him for his own experiences with pigs. Still we said not a word, and presently he was sitting between us opposite the fire, looking anxiously from one of us to the other with a pathetically curious expression. Beyond his first remark that we had been shipwrecked, he had tried to show no interest in where we had come from. As I watched him, I found myself thinking what an ally he would make. He could go where he pleased without having to explain his absence from home to anyone, except his cow and his cats. He was not a gossip, as far as I could judge. And he was a man of ideas, who would understand our wish to save the colt and the filly for Pat. His enthusiasm for the fish factory had proved that, though I had laughed at him for it.

"Pat," I said, "I think we should tell Mr. Faherty what happened to us. Maybe he could help us now."

11

WE MAKE A VALUABLE FRIEND

"Don't say 'Mr. Faherty.' Call me Luke. It's more friendly like."

He hitched himself forward on his little stool and cocked his head on one side hopefully, like a dog that guesses he is going to be brought out after sheep. He looked so friendly that Pat made up his mind to trust him. But first he made Luke promise that he would keep everything we told him secret. Luke would have promised anything, just then.

While we told him the story of our landing on the island and finding the horses, and of our abduction by the two men disguised as Guards, he kept on giving little jumps and squeaks of excitement, very funny to

watch. The cats were displeased at this undignified be-
havior. One by one they moved stiffly away from him,
until they were sitting in a disapproving half-circle at
some distance from the fire.

"And now we don't know what to do," Pat finished.
"We want to go back to the Island of Horses to get the
filly, but we have no boat. And if we had a boat, same,
there would still be the grandmother. She'll lose her life
if we go without her. And then there's the colt. I told
that big thief on the nobbie where he was to be found.
We hardly know where to begin, and that's a fact."

"Begin by going to the Guards," said Luke.

My heart sank. Pat's eyes blazed for a second and
went blank again. Luke saw the effect of his suggestion
as clearly as if we had shouted at him.

"Wait a minute," he said persuasively. "Supposing
those two men are washed up hereabouts, wouldn't it be
nice and handy if the Guards arrested them?"

"On what grounds?" I asked doubtfully.

"For impersonating Guards, of course," said Luke.
"Our Guards' blood will boil at the thought, and they'll
spare no effort to find those two. They'll ask for help
from the Guards in Roundstone and Carraroe and
Clifden, and all along the coast. They'll be mighty busy
fellows until they catch them. An idle mind is the devil's
workshop," he finished solemnly.

It was a good plan, as we could see now. If the
Guards got to the Island of Horses before us, they
would certainly impound all the horses until they could
discover which were stolen and which were wild. As

Luke pointed out, the filly would be a grandmother by the time the law would have come around to handing her back to Pat. He said that he knew Mike Coffey well and had often wondered why he looked more like a pirate than a peddler. One doesn't have a face like Mike's for nothing, said Luke.

"As for a boat," he went on, "I have my own pookaun below at the quay. She's small, but she's handy. Last night's little wind wouldn't have knocked a feather out of her. She'll go to the Island of Horses fine."

"How far is it to the quay?" asked Pat abruptly.

" 'Tis an Irish mile," said Luke, "but we'll step out and we won't be long getting there. The Guards' barracks is handy to the quay, right in the middle of the village."

The village was Kilmoran. I had never been there before, but I had often seen the little group of houses, white and pink, from far out at sea on a day's fishing. We covered the fire with ashes and shut all the cats into the house. Then we started out to the main road for Kilmoran.

It was a long, rough, sandy road, with the sea on our right hand and the mountains on our left. A quarter of a mile from Luke's house we came to a place where a few acres of sour land had been wrenched from the mountain. A clump of fuchsia and thorn bushes concealed a long, low, whitewashed house. We had walked half-way up the boreen toward it when Luke stopped and trumpeted:

"Are you there, Mrs. Joyce, ma'am? Are you there?"

A neat, middle-aged woman with a humorous face appeared in the doorway. She called out, on a high note like a curlew:

"I'm here, Luke. Don't you know well I'm always here?"

"Will you milk the cow for me, Mrs. Joyce, ma'am, and feed the cats, and don't let the fire go out. I'm off for a few days' gallivanting. And there's food for them three robbers of pigs you have in the tub by the back door. And don't leave the cow in the cabbage. And don't leave the big cats drink all the milk on the small cats. And don't leave the door open by night, or I'll come back to find the fox sitting by the fire like any Christian. And lock up your own chicken-house before you go. Did I tell you I saw the fox, Mrs. Joyce, ma'am, as bold as a parson, watching me milking the cow? Did I tell you that?"

"You did, Luke, you did," called Mrs. Joyce. "And I'll go over now and do everything that's wanted."

"Don't go washing my kitchen table," shouted Luke. "It takes the natural oil out of the wood. And don't leave the children near the cats, for fear they'd bite them."

The last piece was an afterthought. It was not at all clear whether Luke feared that the cats would bite the children or the children would bite the cats. The Widow Joyce just laughed and waved us on our way. As we marched briskly back to the main road, Luke said:

"She's a good woman and a good neighbor."

We had difficulty in keeping pace with him, for he moved with a kind of long spring, like a mountain goat.

Still, this was probably a good thing for us, for we were forced to use our stiff muscles to the utmost. By the time we reached Kilmoran we were warm with the exercise, and our fingers and toes were tingling.

The sun was high now, round and clear in a blue sky. Kilmoran village was on a tiny gulf, with the houses in a semicircle facing the sparkling sea. Right in the middle, as Luke had said, was the Guards' barracks. It was a new, white, two-storied building, with a little walled-in garden in front. At one side of the path there was a little patch of smooth grass, and lying coiled up on the grass, like a cow in a field, was an immense Guard. He was fast asleep, breathing gently and peacefully, his huge face flushed and shiny.

"Look at that," said Luke softly, leaning his elbows on the garden wall. "What it is to have a clear conscience!" Suddenly he bawled out: "Johnny! Johnny! The French have landed and the barracks is on fire!"

The big Guard leaped to his feet in one terrible bound. He whirled around, wild-eyed and frantic, and then he saw Luke. At once his expression changed to one of extreme sheepishness, and he said in a very small voice:

"Ah, now, Luke, boy, you have no right to be frightening people like that."

"Come inside," said Luke softly, "and I'll frighten you worse. Where's the Sergeant?"

"He's below in Geraghty's shop buying tobacco. He's a terror for the pipe."

They sent Pat down to fetch the Sergeant while the

rest of us went into the day room. I was very nervous until they came back, for I feared that we would not be able to tell our story without giving away too much information. But I need not have worried. The Sergeant was a thin, stiff-faced man, who did not believe in encouraging boys. He asked Luke to tell the story and only asked us an easy question or two afterward, in a friendly tone, but a little patronizing.

As Luke had predicted, the thought of anyone wearing their uniform for criminal purposes filled them with cold rage. They promised themselves and us that they would leave no stone unturned until they would find those two men, dead or alive. So that they could get started on the hunt at once, they urged Luke to take us down to the quay and sail us back to Inishrone in his pookaun.

Nothing could have suited us better. We left them taking their weapons down from the wall, and skipped outside.

On such a fine day there were few men about. Most of them had gone to the bog or to the fields. But there were plenty of women, and it seemed to me that every one of them came out to watch us embark. Some of them stood in their doorways as if they were only enjoying the morning sun. Others pretended to be hurrying to the shop. But a solid little block of them marched down to the quay. They looked us over from head to toe. They gazed into Luke's boat as if they had never seen it before. They remarked to each other on the absence of lobster pots and fishing nets. They said they had not noticed us land. They said our clothes were made of the island cloth, not the Aran one, but the Inishrone one. They said that Luke looked like a man that was going to do something very important. Luke never once glanced at them, but I could see drops of sweat on his forehead as he hauled up the little sail of the pookaun. Just as we were about to cast off, a fat woman with a face like a duck pushed herself forward to the edge of the quay and said sweetly:

"Luke, agrá, if you're going to the island, maybe you'd bring me with you. I won't take up no more room than a child, and I'll be a help to you if the wind gets fresh, for I'm handy with a boat, so I am."

Luke looked pointedly at the girth of her huge red flannel skirt and said:

"No, thanks. 'Tis real nice of you to offer, Maggie. But I'd have to put the ballast overboard first."

With that we cast off, leaving Maggie in a transport of fury on the quay, surrounded by her chuckling neighbors.

Although there was a useful breeze, the sun shone so brightly that we could see the quiet stones on the floor of the sea. We were all irritated at having to sit back peacefully in a boat instead of charging to attack our enemies. Luke was the worst of us. He kept hopping up and down the pookaun, adjusting ropes and studying the angle of the wind in a fury of impatience. Still he insisted that every move of ours retarded the boat's progress. We did everything that he told us to do, and at last he sat down on a thwart and sighed deeply.

"You surely think I'm touched in the head," he said simply.

We assured him that we did not, though I must admit that I had begun to wonder whether such an excitable man wouldn't prove to be more of a hindrance than a help.

"A grown man has a right to have more sense than I have," Luke went on helplessly. "I do love to be going off like this without warning. But that's only part of it. You see, this won't be my first visit to the Island of Horses. Don't look so disappointed," he said kindly. " 'Tis true that hardly anyone goes there. It's more than twenty years since I was there myself, and I got such a fright that I never went back. Ghosts of horses, appearing from nowhere—that's what frightened me. I never told a soul about it before, for fear they'd be laughing at me. 'Twas curiosity sent me out there in the first place. But I near wrecked the old boat trying to land, and it wasn't until the next morning that I got her off again. I never left the quay all the night. It was dead black. You couldn't see your hand before your face. I fell asleep in the boat, and out in the middle of the night I was waked up by the sound of horses whinnying and hooves galloping above the noise of the wind. My hair stood up straight, I don't mind telling you. I thought my last hour had come."

"And what did you do?"

"I said my prayers," said Luke simply. "Oh, it made a religious man of me, and no mistake. I got away the next day. The wind dropped a small bit at the turn of the tide. But until I met a man sailing out from Kilmoran quay and he passed me the time of day, I wasn't sure was it myself or my ghost."

He said this so solemnly that we dared not laugh. Besides, we were remembering our own terror when we heard the horses gallop past the old forge on our first night on the island. Pat said:

"So there were wild horses there more than twenty years ago. And that was long before Mike Coffey came to these parts."

According to Mike himself, he had been helping to run New York State until the time, about ten years ago, when he had decided to return to Ireland to end his days. Pat was deeply satisfied at Luke's story. Now that the last little doubt was gone, we realized that we had not wholly believed in the survival of the wild horses over all those years.

We were making for Rossmore first, to warn Corny O'Shea to redouble his guard on the colt. Now in that wild part, where there was no shelter from any land, the boat began to get lively. As she climbed and plunged and creaked, every muscle in my body became strained with fear. I thought to myself, I don't know this boat. She looks very old. Probably Luke does not spend much time in repairing her. He's too busy writing letters about his fish factory. He knows how to handle a boat, all right. But I never heard a boat make those noises before. Why is that block knocking? And the jib is so tattered that the sea gulls could fly through the holes in it. And heaven knows when the timber was tarred.

Anxiously and furtively, I looked to see if water was seeping in. Was that a shine among the stones?

At this point I looked across at Pat and was astonished to see him, with wide-open, staring eyes, darting quick, terrified glances about the boat, and then across to the mainland. It dawned upon me that I must look the same, for all to see. Shame-faced, I lifted my eyes to look at Luke. From the far end of the boat he was watching the two of us with pity.

"Indeed and I'm one stupid man," he said bitterly. "After what ye two lads suffered last night, to bring ye out in an open boat on a breezy day and expect ye to enjoy it!"

"We're not like this every day," said Pat, with a poor attempt at a laugh.

He ended with a long, wavering sound like a sea gull's cry, as a tiny splash of spray flipped on to his hand, where it rested on the gunwale. I jumped at the sound, and set the pookaun rocking. A moment later we were both crouched on the bottom of the boat.

"Stay there, let ye," said Luke, "till the fright wears off ye; and we'll sing an old song to pass the time."

"Sing?" we croaked in unison, hardly believing our ears.

"That's right," said Luke kindly. " 'Tis the best cure I know for fright. I'll lead off, and ye can join in as soon as ye're able."

And he started off on a song that we knew well, about a wandering laborer who scorned to work regularly for the strong farmers that came on horseback to

hire him. At the end of the third verse Luke looked so
hurt at our silence that I joined in from politeness. He
had a high, surprisingly musical voice, and he sang the
song with great energy. At the end of it he began the
next one without a pause. It was a song whose chorus
said over and over, with mounting fury: " 'Tis a pity, a
pity, a pity, that I'm not married to Paddy!" Pat joined
in this one, and before we were half-way through we
were shouting as vehemently as ever the writer of that
song could have hoped. At the end, Luke started the
same song again, since it was such a success. Then we
began to remember other songs that we ourselves wanted
to sing. By the time we reached Rossmore, we had long
forgotten our fears and were quite unwilling to stop our
concert.

We did not sail boldly into Rossmore quay. There
were some boats there, but though there was no movement about them, still we were afraid to risk having to
make long explanations which might delay us. A hundred yards west of the quay, Luke slipped the boat in
among the big rocks, as easily as if he were halting a
horse.

"It's dinnertime," he said. "There's no one will come
this way for a while. Let the two of ye lie low in the
boat until I come back. Ye'll be safer here. I'll run up
to Corny O'Shea's house and tell him to shift the colteen
to a better place. I'll hear a bit of news, too, ye may be
sure."

He skipped ashore before we had time to answer and
clambered off up the rough foreshore without once look-

ing back. Pat and I looked at each other helplessly.

"Does he know where Corny's house is?" I said after a moment.

"Yes. Don't you remember, he asked us that particularly when we were telling him the story."

The wait for his return was like to kill us. We watched the sea for boats coming to Rossmore from the islands, and we watched the land for signs of curious people coming down to have a look at our boat. We were watching too for signs that Luke had betrayed us. I believe that until the moment, a long hour later, when he appeared on the shore again alone, we should not have been surprised to find that he was a friend of Mike Coffey. During that hour we had plenty of time to think. Now it occurred to us that we had trusted Luke on very little evidence. Only the evening before, we had handed ourselves over to two strangers who had nearly made an end of us.

"Oh, Danny, when will we get sense?" said Pat. " 'Tisn't brains we have in our heads, but porridge, or soup, or sawdust. Maybe we should push off this old boat this minute and go to the Island of Horses alone."

But I defended Luke.

"Look at the open, honest face of him, compared with the other two," I said. "Think of the big flow of talk out of him. Everything he said showed what kind of a man he is."

"That's true," Pat remembered. "If he was a friend of Mike Coffey, he'd throw the old potatoes behind the fire rather than keep them for anyone's pigs."

"And Mrs. Joyce was as honest as the sun," said I, "and she seemed to be great friends with him."

It was at that moment that we saw Luke climbing down over the rocks toward us. It was well that we had reached this point in our discussion, for he looked us over sharply as if to see if we were still friendly. What he saw must have pleased him. He boarded the boat and shoved off at once, with his usual jerky energy. We asked no questions, but got up sail as fast as we could. She filled with the good southwesterly breeze.

"Now," said Luke, "to Inishrone to fetch the grandmother and then straight for the Island of Horses!"

12

THE GRANDMOTHER GOES
SAILING AGAIN

While he was telling us the news of his visit to Corny, Luke kept on taking chunks of soda-bread out of his pockets. He had two small pieces of bacon as well, with the compliments of Mrs. O'Shea, and she was sorry we had not come up with Luke for a proper dinner.

"Oh, she's a fine, decent woman," he said. "She had me sitting down at the table before I was two minutes in the house and a mountain of food before me, like what would be put before Finn MacCool in the old stories. Let ye eat up now, and I'll be telling ye what I heard."

There was a strong smell of old fish on the bread—this came from Luke's pockets. Indeed everything about

Luke smelled of fish, as if he were a seal. We cared nothing for that, of course, and we were very thankful to him for bringing us the food.

"The first thing to tell you is that the colt is safe and sound," Luke began. "They shifted him this morning to a sheep cave on the mountain. Mrs. O'Shea's nephew, Batty Kelly, is with him, and they want for nothing."

"Why did they shift him?" Pat asked at once.

"Because your father was over at the crack of dawn this morning, looking for the two of you," said Luke. "They all said that you wouldn't willingly have gone away so soon without saying a word to anyone. They said your going away might have something to do with the colt, so they moved him into hiding, just to be on the safe side."

"What did my father do when there was no sign of us at Rossmore?" Pat asked softly.

"He didn't like it," said Luke emphatically. "He did not, and that's the truth. It seems that some island man saw the strange nobbie making off toward Rossmore, as he thought. He didn't watch her for long, he says, because he was walking away from Garavin and he got tired of turning his head. He wouldn't have noticed her at all, he says, but for the way she was beating the sea with her tail, like a basking shark or a sea pig that would be giving warning of a storm."

"The blessings of God on him," said Pat a little impatiently. "Did my father say what he was going to do?"

"He said he would go back to Inishrone and get all the island men to come out in their boats after the nobbie. Corny O'Shea said to that, that it would be more sensible to get the Guards after it in the lifeboat. So the pair of them went down to the barracks to see the Sergeant. I'll have a small tasteen of that bit of bread you have, boy," he said to me, in a tone suddenly apologetic.

I broke off a piece and handed it to him without a word. By this time Pat's hand was clutching at the front of his own jersey, as if it were alive independently of its owner. His face was wrinkled up with a fury of impatience. Luke, examining his piece of bread with appreciation, seemed not to notice. I said hastily:

"What did the Sergeant say?"

"The Sergeant got out the lifeboat, decent enough, and they coasted up and down for a whileen until—"

"Until what?"

"Until they found the mast of a nobbie washed up on the rocks off Lettermullen. But they found nothing but only the mast alone," he went on quickly. He had seen at once the thought that had flashed into our minds. "There was a rope around it, a long, trailing sort of a rope, like it would be opened out by your two friends when they landed."

"And what did my father make of that?" Pat asked very quietly.

"He made out that it was no more use to be looking for you," said Luke. "The Sergeant was more hopeful. It was he that said it looked as if the mast had been used as a kind of a lifebuoy. They all went up to the barracks at Lettermullen, and the Sergeant got his people to start a search for anyone that might have been washed up by the tide. In about an hour's time they found your two friends drinking poteen in a mountainy man's house, mighty sorry for themselves, and saying very nasty things about Mike Coffey."

"About Mike! Did they name him to the Guards?"

"Name him?" Luke laughed with pleasure. "As far as I can judge, any name they didn't put on him wouldn't be worth a tinker's damn. They told the Guards that you'd need a very good boat for the kind of job they were on last night. They said that Mike Coffey ought to be in jail for sending them out in such a bad boat. They said it was their misfortune to be so tall, for that is why Mike picked them for the job, because the uniforms fitted them so nice. Oh, they make powerful poteen in the mountains, and no mistake. After one mug of it you'd be talking about your mother's people, and after two you'd confess to causing the San Francisco fire."

Though we had gone to some trouble to send the Kilmoran Guards after the two men, we were not at all pleased that they had been captured so soon.

"Did you hear at all what their names are," I asked now, "or where they came from?"

"They're Kerrymen, or so they told the Guards. That's Mike Coffey's country too." By the tone of Luke's voice it was easy to see that he expected no better of Kerrymen. "They called each other Foxy and Joe. That was all the names I heard on them."

"And where are they now?"

"On their way in to Galway. They're going to be charged with stealing the Guards' uniforms, though no one knows yet where they got them. That will do for a start. There will be other things later. Oh, we won't be seeing them for some time, I'm thinking."

"And Mike Coffey? What is going to be done about him?"

"There will be a big search started for Mike Coffey," said Luke slowly. "Sooner or later that search will lead to the Island of Horses. We must make it our business to get there before the Guards, or it will be all up with our chances of getting your filly and bringing her home."

"So you think the Guards will go to the Island of Horses?" said Pat after a moment.

"I don't know what to think, and that's the truth," said Luke helplessly. "All I can say is that the sooner we get there and take away what we want from it, the better. After that we won't care who goes there or how long they stay."

That was sense, as we could see. Luke's old boat was doing her best. For all her creaking and groaning, her tattered sails and splintered timbers, she was skimming over the shining sea as eagerly as if this were her first voyage. Luke managed her like a master. With no more than a lift of his finger, he made every ounce of wind work for him. His skill was a joy to watch, and presently Pat paid him the highest compliment he could think of:

"Luke, you're as good in a boat as my brother John."

Luke showed all his strong, white teeth in a delighted smile. Presently I asked:

"Did you hear any word at all about Mike Coffey himself? Or where did he go when he left Inishrone yesterday?"

"He came to Rossmore, they say," said Luke. "He left Andy in the boat and went up to Stephen Costelloe's shop for a while. He drank a pint of porter and bought a box of matches for his pipe. Stephen served him himself and walked down to the quay with him afterward. Mike sailed off with Andy, west in the Clifden direction, and he hasn't been seen since."

"I never heard that Mike and Stephen Costelloe were friendly," said Pat doubtfully.

"Mrs. O'Shea said they were as thick as thieves yesterday," said Luke. He stopped suddenly. "As thick as thieves? Did you hear what I said? There's many a true word spoken in jest. I bet you fourpence that Stephen Costelloe is mixed up somehow in Mike's horse business, whatever it is."

But Pat would not believe that. He said that Stephen was mean, as all the world knew, but that he was never dishonest. Luke shook his head.

"From what I've seen in the world," he said, " a mean man falls into every kind of badness sooner or later. He learns to put everything right with his conscience, to suit himself. He ends up with no conscience at all, or one with a skin on it like an eel, tough and slippery. Mind you, I'm not saying Stephen is a horse thief. From what I hear, he's so wealthy he doesn't have to bother.

But there's plenty of other things he could be doing that wouldn't bear the light of day."

"What kind of things?" Pat asked sharply.

"I'm thinking you could make a few suggestions yourself," said Luke.

He closed his mouth firmly, as if to make certain that he would say no more. Pat fell into a long silence. I could see that he was turning over and over what Luke had said and trying to see into Stephen Costelloe's little, twisted brain.

For my part, I soon gave up attempting to understand what Stephen was planning. Now at last we were approaching Inishrone. Sitting back in the stern of the boat, I watched the island grow clearer with every yard that we travelled. Gradually the scattered white specks became houses, and the haze of grey became a network of stone walls around rocky fields. Next I could see trailing veils of smoke from the chimneys, scattering through the bright air.

We did not go in to the quay at Garavin. As we came close in, we could see a forest of masts there, as if every boat belonging to the island was in the harbor. We sailed along the length of the island instead, to a little cove among the rocks below Conroys' house. Conroy's coracle was there, drawn up on the stony beach. The sun had moved around, leaving the cove in shadow. A sort of natural slip of rocks ran out a little way into the sea, and we made fast there, in deep water, and sprang ashore.

"Off with the two of ye now," said Luke, "and fetch the grandmother. I'll stay here with the old boat. And bring a bite of food back with ye, if ye can," he called after us hoarsely as we started up the shore. "And for the love of Mike don't let the old woman break her leg on them rocks. They'd lame a young hardy one, not to mind an old woman of eighty years of age—"

"We'll look after her well," said Pat.

We skipped over the rocks and away out of sight as fast as we could, so that he could give us no more instructions. Though he had indeed tried to lower his voice, he had quite failed in it.

There were no houses on this part of Inishrone. It faced directly into the Atlantic Ocean, so that for many months of the year it had no shelter from the storms. After each storm the foreshore looked different, with the huge rocks all rearranged by the giant hands of the sea. At the top of the shore we followed an old road of rough stones until we came up on to a long, grassy slope. The grass was delightfully soft on our bare feet after the stones. There were a few sheep there now for the summer. Already they had cropped the grass short.

At the top of the slope we paused. We could see the back to Conroys' house from here. The back door was shut. The hens were all in the little walled yard. I pointed this out to Pat.

"Does that mean there's no one at home?" I asked.

"Yes," said Pat. "My mother always shuts them in like that when she's leaving the house. If she was at home those hens would be picking around the front door and watching their chance to slip into the kitchen. We're in luck."

"Will the grandmother be there, though?" I asked doubtfully, for the place looked very deserted.

"The grandmother is always there," said Pat.

We had to cross two fields before we reached the house. We kept under the shadow of its walls until we came to the gable. After that it was no use hiding any longer. With one quick glance down the boreen toward the road, we slipped around the corner to the front door.

I would not have been surprised to have found the big door closed, as it was at night or when everyone had gone out. But now we saw that only the half-door was shut, so that we were able to look over the top into the kitchen. On the opposite wall, the delft on the dresser glowed like fire in the slanting afternoon sun. The rest of the room was dim by comparison. Even the firelight seemed to have faded. Pat pushed the door open abruptly, and we went inside.

The grandmother was sitting in her usual place on the hob. She started when she saw us. She had been saying her prayers, and in her surprise her huge black rosary beads clattered to the floor. Pat stooped to pick them up for her. She put out her hand and touched his forehead gently. Then she gave a terrible, slow sigh.

"There was never one of our family drowned yet, Patcheen," she said. "Never a one. I didn't want you to start the fashion."

"Where are they all?" Pat asked softly.

"Off to Garavin. God grant your father won't meet Mike Coffey, or there will be murder done. Himself and John came back in here an hour ago and took down the guns that they have for shooting seals. After they were gone, your mother and the girls were around the house here like hens when the fox would be sniffing about the place. 'Twas I told them they'd best be off into Garavin after the men, and that I'd stay here and pray for all sinners. How is it you didn't see them in Garavin?" she asked suddenly.

"We didn't go in to Garavin. We landed below at Cuandubh. There's a man from over Kilmoran way with us. He's minding the boat. He's a good man. You'd nearly take him for an island man. He's coming with us now to the Island of Horses."

She looked sharply from one of us to the other.

"You're going to the Island of Horses now?"

"We must go there, to take away a little wild filly that we saw there," said Pat. "We came to bring you with us. Will you come?"

For a second she looked frightened. Then she stood up slowly. Almost as if she were talking in her sleep, she said:

"Yes. Yes. I'll come with you. To the Island of Horses. I said I wanted to go there. I said that, and you didn't forget it." She went to the dresser and took down a fat white china jug with roses on it. Out of the jug she took a key on a long string and handed it to Pat. "Open the chest for me, Patcheen, agrá, till I get out my shawl."

Pat unlocked the carved chest that stood by the back door. It had always been an object of curiosity to me, and I moved forward with the others to peer into it. Right on top, neatly folded, was a dark-brown habit such as I had often seen on dead people at wakes. The grandmother gave a little happy laugh when she saw it.

"Look at that," she said. "I was full sure that that would be the next bit of finery I'd wear. Lift it out carefully, Patcheen. I don't want there to be any wrinkles in it. Now just hand me the shawl." Pat took out a beautiful pale-brown shawl, bordered with flowers in darker brown, pale green, and red. "And there's a clean checked apron below that. Now put back the habit carefully."

Pat did as she said. He locked the chest again and gave her the key. She made us turn away while she chose a different jug in which to hide it. Then she put on the clean blue-and-white checked apron over her red petticoat, and put the soft, fine shawl around her shoulders.

"I'm ready now," she said simply.

We took a new loaf of soda-bread out of the corner press and some cold boiled potatoes that had been kept for the hens. These we tied up in an old flour bag, with a little parcel of meal to make porridge. Then we put some turf on the fire, and we were ready to go.

We each took one of the old woman's arms to help her along. I could feel her whole body shake under my fingers, and I had a moment of panic at what we were doing. As if she had read my thoughts, she said:

"Don't trouble yourself about me, Danny. I'll be all right in a whileen. 'Tis a queer long time since I went for a walk, that's all."

We took her by the way that we had come, up through the two fields and out onto the grassy slope that now stretched away down to the shore. Our progress was slow, of course.

It was when we were going down the long slope among the sheep that I noticed that someone was watching us. A head had popped up from behind the wall of the field that we had just left. I had glanced backward just then, for no good reason, and was just in time to see it drop down out of sight again. Whoever was there could easily observe us still, of course, through any of the stones in the loosely built stone wall. I said nothing to Pat. It was no use trying to hurry the grandmother. It would have been very false economy to have made her trot now and perhaps have her collapse before we would reach the boat.

Half a dozen times before we came to the shore I looked back toward the ridge. Pat noticed it at last. So did the grandmother.

"There isn't a soul in this part of the island today, Danny," she said. "They're all congregated below in Garavin, breaking their hearts over two young lads that's well able to mind themselves."

But Pat looked anxiously at me, and I could see that he guessed I was not fretting without reason. He asked no questions, however.

Down on the rocky road that ran along the top of the

shore, we half carried the old woman between us. She leaned very heavily on us now, and the beautiful shawl kept slipping off her shoulders. When we had covered half of the distance from the shore to the boat, she stopped and said:

"I'm afraid I'm too old to be gallivanting. Old women should sit on the hob and knit socks. That's all they're fit for."

" 'Tis as easy for you to go on as to go back," Pat coaxed her.

I looked back again, and this time I saw the head and shoulders of the person who was following us, just before they disappeared out of sight behind a rock. It was a woman. I felt a little glow of relief. I was still young enough then to think that women are poor, weak creatures that would not hurt a fly. I joined with Pat in encouraging the grandmother to come with us the last little piece of the way. She said, quite sharply:

"Of course I'll come. Do you think you could leave me after you now? 'Tis only old talk with me. My head is as young as your own. 'Tis only the legs that are old."

And she dragged herself along valiantly again.

As soon as we came in sight of the pookaun, Luke came hopping over the rocks to help us. When we reached the place where we must leave the road and start down the shore to the boat, he said:

"Excuse me, Mrs. Conroy, ma'am, for what I'm going to do."

And without ceremony he swept her up in his arms

and carried her down over the beach as easily as he would have carried a creel of seaweed. She gave one sharp yelp, and no more. Pat and I walked on either side of Luke, in terror lest he drop her. We could see that she was not too heavy, but her voluminous clothes cut off his view of the ground. Every moment we feared that he would step into one of the deep crannies among the rocks and come crashing down with his load. I must admit that our chief fear was of what we would say to Pat's father if we failed to return his mother safe and sound. Still I think we feared the old woman more, for we would not have dreamed of setting off without her, once she had said she wanted to come with us.

We soon saw that Luke knew what he was about. Guided by some instinct, he set his feet always in the right places. He did not even seem short of breath as he explained:

"I often have to go down to the sea in the night time. That's why I had to get good at this class of thing. You're not afraid, Mrs. Conroy, ma'am?" he finished anxiously.

"No," said the old woman, firmly enough. "I'm not afraid."

Right by the pookaun, he set her down carefully. She smoothed her apron, brushed back her white hair with the palms of her hands, and drew her shawl firmly around her. Then she looked back toward the way that we had come and said sweetly:

"I must thank you heartily, Luke, for the help you gave me. Anyone would think you spent your days

carrying women up and down the strand, so they
would." Suddenly she gave a little cry and pointed with
her finger. "Arrah, will you look who's here to wish me
Godspeed! You can come out from behind that rock,
Miss Doyle, and bid us the time of day like a lady!"

We all looked, and I was hard put to it not to burst
out laughing. Out from behind a rock, sure enough,
came the elder Miss Doyle. She looked as remote and
as queenly as ever, though she was limping after her
long walk from the other end of the island. So far as I
knew, neither herself nor her sister had ever left Garavin on foot before. Once or twice they had paid a royal
visit to our house and to the others in our neighborhood, coming in a sidecar. She looked a sorry figure
now, with her hair in wisps, and a tear in her coat, and
the heel off one shoe. I felt a surge of resentment against
her for the fright she had given me.

"What brings you here?" I asked roughly. "What are
you following us for? You'd best be off home now and
don't tell anyone what you saw, or it will be the worse
for you!"

"You are a very rude boy," she said sourly. "I'll tell
your father about you the next time I see him."

"Run away home, ma'am," said Luke impatiently,
"and don't be wasting our time."

"Who is this man?" she demanded of Pat. "And why
is he abducting Mrs. Conroy?"

"Abducting your granny!" said the old woman. "I'm
just going out for a sail in a pookaun. Now let you be

off home, like a good girl, or you'll be caught by the darkness on the way."

But she would not move. After a moment Luke said: "Well, boys, we have no time to lose. Into the boat, now."

Miss Doyle watched us silently while Luke got on board and we handed the grandmother down to him. While we were casting off, Miss Doyle came right over to peer down into the boat. We could not have stopped her except perhaps by pelting her with stones, and of course we could not do that to a woman. We said as much to the grandmother, for it was she who had suggested this method of getting rid of the unwelcome member of the party.

"I'm sorry for ye," said the grandmother, with a contemptuous sniff.

Miss Doyle stood so close to the boat that it occurred to me that she might try to leap on board at the last moment, just as we pushed off. I could not imagine why she should do this, nor indeed why she was so much interested in us at all. She made no move, however, until we were a yard or so out from the reef. Then we saw her clambering along to the end to watch us sail away. She stayed there, like a cormorant on a rock, until we were three hundred yards out to sea. Then we saw her hurry back along the reef, with a strange, flopping motion, until we lost sight of her among the huge rocks.

13

BACK TO THE ISLAND
OF HORSES

"Who is that poor, daft creature?" Luke asked. "She looks like someone that's after spending her life behind a counter."

We told him that Miss Doyle and her sister kept the post office in Garavin.

"I thought as much," he said with a wise nod. "Post offices always bring out the worst in people."

" 'Tis true," said Mrs. Conroy. "But she's not daft at all. She's bad. I could see with my own two eyes that the divil is on her."

None of us had the least idea as to why she had come to spy on us. Luke said:

"I'm sorry we couldn't lead her astray a bit about the

direction we're going in. But sure, there's only the two
directions—northwest to the Island of Horses and south-
east back to Garavin, and we couldn't go that way for
fear we'd be seen. Bad luck to her, anyway, and that's
all I say."

Though we tried to forget her after that, still she had
left us with an uneasy feeling. As long as we could see
the shore that we had left, Pat and I kept watching it
as if we expected an army to appear on it at any moment. But not so much as a bird stirred there. When at
last we gave it up, we found that the grandmother was
looking at us with a wry smile. She was sitting in the
stern, cushioned on an old sail and wrapped warmly in
her shawl. She seemed perfectly content.

"Now, let ye not spoil the day on me with talk of that
old Miss Doyle," she said. "Ye can do nothing about
her. When ye're my age ye'll maybe have learned not
to lose sleep over things ye can't fix."

And she began to point out landmarks on the far
Connemara coast that she remembered from the days of
her youth, headlands and little islands and reefs. Some
she called by names that we knew, but to others she
gave names that no one uses now.

We caught our first sight of the Island of Horses
while we were still in the shelter of the high cliffs of
Inishrone. The grandmother sat up straight when she
saw it. Her expression was a mixture of love and irrita-
tion. I was reminded of the look that used to come over
my father's face whenever he spoke of our little Kerry
cow. She would break out of every field that she was

put in and send him dancing the length of Inishrone after her. But always in the end he said the same thing, that she was the finest cow on the island and that he would not part with her for gold nor for silver. Old Mrs. Conroy had suffered enough from the Island of Horses, but now it was plain enough that her heart was still there. The question that Pat had begun to ask her faded into silence. Instead, he went astern to arrange the old sail behind her shoulders so that she could lean back comfortably. For the rest of the journey she seemed to lapse into a dream. We took care not to disturb her.

Out on the open sea, we were carried along on a great, blue swell. Even with Luke's presence to give us confidence, it was a frightening journey. The pookaun was just too small and the sea too big. A sweeping wind whistled through the sails. Sometimes it seemed to lift the boat right out of the water, dropping her again to flounder about among the heavy waves. Only a few brave sea gulls followed us.

Gradually the dark blue of the Island of Horses became dark green. The sun was going down somewhere behind it by this time. The sky was streaked with a soft pink haze that stretched away and away as far as we could see. Now the sea had become a little calmer. Luke was the first to break the long silence.

"Where do you think we should land, Mrs. Conroy, ma'am? You know the island better than we do."

"Go in to the quay first," she said quietly. "I want to find the house where I was born."

My heart sank as I remembered the ruins at the quay side. Pat glanced at me, and I could see that he was thinking of the same thing. How easy it seemed now to have left the grandmother safe in the chimney corner of her son's house! But it was no use lamenting over that now, for we were almost in to the quay.

Following Mrs. Conroy's instructions, Luke lowered all sail a hundred yards out.

"Often I watched the men do it," she said, "and never a boat was lost. The time that all the boats were broken up they were tied to the quay wall. We stood up by the houses, watching them banging about. The men crawled down along the quay on their hands and knees, on account of the fierce wind, hoping to be able to save them. God look down on us all! There was no hope of saving them. 'Twould draw tears from a stone to see all the grand boats and they grinding into powder and going down under the water before our eyes."

" 'Twas a black time, God save the mark," said Luke gently.

He let the pookaun glide in to the quay and made her fast. Then we all stepped ashore, holding the grandmother by the hands to help her.

Once on shore, the old woman shook herself gently free of us. She stood still for a minute, looking toward the little huddle of ruins that had been her world. Then, with slow, firm steps, she began to walk toward them.

We followed as closely as we dared. I could hardly breathe. It was as if a huge hand were gripping my chest, crushing my ribs until I gasped with the pain of it. We could not see the old woman's face. She had drawn her shawl up over her head as if she were in church. Only by watching her straight back and the slow swing of her skirts could we guess at the sorrow that was like to overwhelm her.

All up the length of the quay she never paused nor turned her head. Like a sleepwalker she passed the first houses and the old forge where Pat and I had spent our nights on the island. Beyond the forge, where the old road took a turn uphill away from the sea, at the very last house in the village, she stopped. She turned to look at us now, and her wide, dark eyes were full of tears.

"This was our house," she said.

It stood in a little walled field of its own. A clump of nettles grew against the one sheltered gable. Everywhere else there was short, clean grass, kept thus by the bitter, salty winds of winter. She passed through the gap where once there had been a gate, and went to the yawning, empty doorway of the house. She stood in the doorway for a long time. Then, with a sudden brisk movement, she walked into the house. We followed.

She went to the middle of the big room that had been the kitchen and looked upward at the naked gables. Then she walked across to the grassy hearth of the fireplace. Under the shelter of the chimneypiece the hobs were still clean and whitewashed. Very slowly, she moved in and sat down on one of them.

"God be praised," thought I, seeing her gaze wandering from wall to wall of the ruined house, "she's gone queer in the head at last. Oh, why did we not see that this would happen?"

She was talking softly now, almost to herself. I moved a little closer, to hear what she was saying. Pat and Luke were still standing in the doorway. Luke's sharp, weather-beaten face was full of pity. Pat looked a little frightened.

"That's where the holy picture used to be, with a light in front of it always," said the grandmother, pointing to the back wall. "Look, there's the nail, still there. Under that was the settle, where I used to sleep. I used to love the light from the little lamp, and the light from the fire when everyone would be gone away and I'd be here on my lone. Then the crickets used to come out and do their little step-a-kipeen on the hearthstone, and sing me to sleep. The dresser was over there"—she pointed to the opposite wall. "We had the loveliest bowls on the Island of Horses, as everyone knows. Under the window, there, was the table. Many's the fine loaf of soda-bread I made standing at it, with one eye on the work and the other watching out to sea for the boats coming back till we'd have sport and dancing in the nighttime. Oh, that was a grand life and a grand place to live." Suddenly she looked at us straight.

"Don't be afraid," she said. "I'm not gone soft in the head. 'Tis the other way about with me. All the long years that I've been thinking and thinking about this place, I used to wonder to myself if I had made a kind of fairyland of it in my own mind. I used to try to think of ugly things that happened here, to give myself a disgust for the place. But I could never remember anything but fun and laughing and songs, and the little calves in the sunshine, and sunny evenings on the mountain, and fat hens pecking around the door, and the fine, beautiful horses. I used to think there could be no place as fine as the Island of Horses that I remembered. That's why I had to see it again. 'Twas to make sure that I was right all the time." She laughed happily. "And I was right. There's no place in the whole wide world like the Island of Horses!"

Now we knew that she was as sensible as ourselves. Luke said:

" 'Tis the truest word you ever spoke, Mrs. Conroy, ma'am. And a sore thing it must have been to leave it all behind."

The old woman nodded slowly. Neither Pat nor I said a word. All at once, it seemed as if the grass and the nettles had disappeared, and in their places had come all the little things that make up an island kitchen—the churn and the creepie stools, the carved chests and dresser, and the settle bed, all held in the soft, warm glow of the turf fire and of the oil lamp on the wall. It seemed so real that when I looked upward I almost expected to find that the rafters had grown again, and that a stout thatch roof would shelter us for the night. But all I saw was the big round moon in a greenish-blue sky, still full of daylight, looking down curiously into the ruin. The grandmother said:

"Anyone that would see us now would think we were daft, playing house at this hour of the evening." She stood up. "I'm fine and rested now. We'd best be getting on with the work."

For all her brave words, it seemed as if she had grown smaller and more feeble since we had landed on the Island of Horses. As we walked back to the quay, she allowed Luke to hold her arm. We were glad of this, for she stumbled a little, more than once.

We had decided to sail around to the silver strand, to save the old woman the labor of walking there. The pookaun drew very little water, and it would be an easy matter to run her up on the sand. We would catch the filly at once and lead her on board. Then, under cover of darkness, we would sail across to the strand below Luke's house where we had been wrecked.

"I have a nice, dry little stable," said Luke. "The old jackass will move over and give the filly room. And sure, if she's too grand to stay with him, she'll be welcome inside in my own house."

This was a handsome offer. We accepted it gratefully on behalf of the filly.

"I'll consult herself about the food she'll have," said Luke.

The tide had turned, and the boat had risen an inch or two since we had left her. Over where we had caught the eels, the sea was flowing in over the soft sand. In the ruined village the walls of the houses made a black, jagged pattern against the sky. The air had chilled when the sun went down. Now a little night wind moaned and whistled through the holes in our old sails. Then, away off in the distance, the long joyful whinny of a horse was carried to us on the breeze. The grandmother gave a little, happy laugh at the sound.

She instructed us to keep well out to sea while we were rounding the end of the island.

"There's long reefs there, just under the water," she said. "They only show in the low spring tides."

Presently we passed by the long silver strand. At the far end of it the cliffs came around in a wide semicircle toward the sea, and then we saw the smaller strand with the long, flat valley behind it. We turned in toward it. At the base of the cliff we ran the pookaun in on to the sand. Just as she grounded, Luke hopped into the water and hauled her up high and dry. He moored her by a long rope to an outcropping rock at the foot of the cliff. There was a little cave there, in the cliff's face, with the water already lapping at its door.

Pat and I sprang ashore. The grandmother insisted on coming with us, though we tried to persuade her to stay by the boat. Up over the long strand we went, until we came to the wild, rough grass that grew at the edge of the valley. Even in the few days since we had been here the sea pinks had begun to flower.

A little mist was gathering over the grass. It was almost night. We stood still, and then we made out the shapes of the horses in the dimness. They were still, too, watching us. Then one of them began to move toward us, first at a sharp walking pace, then at a trot, and at last cantering over the grass with flying hooves and mane. A shiver of fear went through me.

"It's the black stallion!" I shouted.

Luke put out his hands and drew us all together, so that we stood in a huddled group. Still the stallion came on. Then, a few yards away from us, he wheeled in a great circle and galloped off up the valley again. We felt the turf shiver under our feet. In the moment when he passed us, with rolling eyes and stretched nostrils, he had seemed to me like a playing porpoise or a good sheep dog stretching his legs on the mountainside.

"We needn't be afraid of him," I said. "I don't believe he means us any harm."

Luke's voice shook a little as he answered:

"I have a great respect for stallions, so I have."

We listened to the huge thunder of his hooves on the hollow-sounding turf. Above the whine of the wind, it was like the wild sound of drums in a distant pipers' band. The blood sang in my ears from the excitement. The hoof beats became louder. He was coming back.

"God be praised!" said Luke. "There's a fellow I'd like to bring home. But 'twould be easier to catch the north wind in a fishnet than to lay a finger on him."

Out of the dusk he came again. He reared on his hind legs and shook his little head until his mane flew about him like smoke. Then he sent a tremendous whinny rolling around the hilltops. His white teeth glittered in the moonlight. This time he circled behind us, before pounding off up the valley again.

Mrs. Conroy sighed. It sounded like a little moan. "I'm an old, old woman," she said in a half-whisper. "It's sixty long years since I led our black stallion down into this valley. He must be long dead and gone, long, long dead. But you'd think 'tis himself is here tonight, and he galloping and wheeling and circling the way he did that day when I left him. I wish I was young again, so I do, and I'd stay on the Island of Horses as long as I'd live."

Pat said:

" 'Tis terrible the grip that this place takes on you. If we stayed here for a week, I'd swear we'd go as wild as the horses ourselves."

"That's a true word," said Luke. " 'Tis like a fairy island."

Then we saw the stallion coming back at an easy trot. He stopped a little distance away, at the edge of the group of horses, and pretended to crop the grass. But we could see that he was keeping a sharp eye on us as well.

Now that the daylight was really gone, the moon and the stars had come into their own. Their soft brilliant light poured into the valley like milk into a bowl. The rocks and the grass and the stream and the gently moving horses had all changed until they looked like things seen in a picture.

Now we wondered how we could ever have thought that all the horses were the same. The wild ones moved with a quick, nervous grace, edging away and away as we approached. The others stood solidly on their four heavy hooves, dragging the grass out by the roots with their great, clumsy teeth and only swishing their tails lazily when we rudely slapped their haunches. We went in and out, through them, looking for the filly. When we saw her at last, she seemed to guess why we had come. She kicked her heels in the air and danced away. But she was too young to have learned the tricks that would have saved her from us. Within five minutes we had surrounded her. She stood, shivering, between us, with Luke's thin, strong rope expertly knotted around her head.

"Easy, there," he said to her, very softly. "You'll get very fond of me yet."

He rubbed her nose over and over. When he stopped this, she moved a little nearer to him.

"See that?" he said, delighted. "I'd swear that's the first time that anyone rubbed her nose for her."

As we led her slowly down toward the strand, the stallion lifted his head and watched us. The grandmother walked with one arm around the filly's neck, leaning on her for support. Though the stallion shook his head and whinnied, he did not follow us. It was almost as if he knew that whatever the old woman did must be right and that but for her he would not be there at all. Luke went at the other side of the filly, and Pat and I followed. Suddenly Pat gave a little chuckle.

"This is a great night's work, Danny," he said. "I'll never forget it the longest day I live."

"What I'll never forget is our first sight of this place," I said. "Do you remember lying up there on the hill? And thinking we should hear the sea?"

As I spoke I had swung around to point to the place on the hilltop from which we had first seen the valley of wild horses. Pat turned too. Then he clutched at my arm and squeezed it so that I felt his fingernails pierce through my thick jersey. I gave a little shriek at the pain of it. Luke stopped.

"What's that? What's that?" he asked sharply.

"Up on top, there." Pat pointed as he gasped for breath. "I saw heads, moving."

"Ha!" said Luke. "Heads, indeed! How many?"

"Two."

From the sound of his voice, I thought that Pat was going to burst into tears. For the first time in my life, I felt that it was I who was the stronger. To be sure, we had shared the whole adventure equally. But here on the island Pat seemed somehow to be weaker, as if the spirits of his ancestors, instead of coming to his aid, were sucking his manhood away.

The grandmother had stopped too, a few paces off. She leaned against the filly still. Luke held the end of the rope. He flicked it quickly about as he turned to me.

"Did you see them too, Danny?"

I explained that I had been trying to pick out the exact spot from which we had first seen the valley. Still I had an impression of something moving, over on the left.

"That's right, Danny," said Pat, a little more firmly. "A round head and a thin one, so thin it looked more like a neck with no head on top."

Luke slapped the end of the rope across his other hand. He gave a little shout of laughter.

"That's the best description of Andy Coffey that I ever heard. A neck with no head on top! 'Tis true for you, indeed, Pat. That's what you saw."

"The Coffeys?"

My insides gave a horrid little bound and seemed to settle somewhere lower down than they should.

"Who else?" said Luke. "Come along, now. No more talk. Save your breath for speed. Maybe we'll be away before they can get around to the strand."

14

MIKE COFFEY MEETS HIS MATCH, AND THE GRANDMOTHER RECEIVES A VISITOR

We kept silent as we continued on our way to the shore. This was not because we were moving quickly, but because we guessed that Luke needed time to think. Indeed our progress was slower now than before, because the grandmother seemed suddenly to have lost the last of her strength. Even walking behind her as I was, I could hear her gasping for breath with a pitiful little crying sound which she could not suppress. She had said nothing about the arrival of the Coffeys on the island. Still I remembered once hearing her say that when one is old one can no longer run from danger, and that it is easier at last to stay and submit to it.

But this would not do for us, and she was trying her best not to be a hindrance to us.

As we went at a snail's pace, I imagined how the Coffeys would have run down to the quay again, and launched their boat, and put to sea, and would even now be on their way to the silver strand. I had no doubt but that they must have seen us, in the sharp, white moonlight.

Presently Luke gave Pat the rope's end to hold, and he and I supported the old woman between us. With infinite kindness he encouraged her to keep going and praised her for each little effort that she made. And when she stopped at last and said we should leave her, he carried her again as he had done on the rough strand at Cuandubh.

The pookaun was afloat when we reached the water's edge. I hauled on her long rope and brought her sliding in until she bumped on the sand. Then Luke said, with a little helpless gesture:

"I'm afraid it won't work, boys. If we all get aboard her here, she'll sink in the sand. It wouldn't matter if we could wait for the tide to come up and float her off."

"The Coffeys will be here long before that could happen," said Pat. "If it wasn't for the filly—"

The grandmother chuckled. It was such an unexpected sound that we all turned toward her. In the clear light of the moon we could discern the same villainous grin with which she always watched the antics of her descendants from the hob in Conroy's kitchen.

"Ha!" she said now, and she thumped her bony hands together with delight. "I thought I'd be a drawback, and a hindrance, and a heartscald to ye. And now I'm going to be useful after all."

"Don't worry your head, Mrs. Conroy, ma'am," said Luke quickly. "The island is big enough, and we'll be hard to catch, I'll warrant you."

By the way he turned his head to look out to sea, I knew how he grudged every moment spent in humoring her.

The old woman saw this too. She pointed to the cave in the face of the cliff.

"If you put myself and the filly into that cave, you'll have two less to look after. The Coffeys will never find us. We'll be as safe as if we were in the body of the jail."

She had our attention now, without a doubt.

"But that cave is surely full of sea water even now," said Luke in despair. "Do you want to be drowned inside in it, God save the mark?"

"There's no more than eighteen inches of water at the mouth of that cave this minute," said the grandmother. "I know it well from the old times. There's a little, small strand in at the back that's never covered but at the spring tides. And I do not want to be drowned, no more than anyone else, but I don't want to go hopping from rock to rock of my own island either, at this hour of my life, with a family of robbers after me. That's what's in store for us all in a few minutes, if you don't get me into that cave in quick time." She turned to Pat and said softly: "I'll mind the filly for you, Patcheen, as if she was my own child. Never fear of that."

Luke gave us the task of leading the filly into the cave. He said that he would take charge of the grandmother. We rolled the legs of our trousers high. Luke did not trouble to do this, for he was already wet up to the knees from bringing the boat ashore.

At first the filly was very reluctant to follow us into the water. We were surprised at this, for we had thought until then that the wild horses probably went for an occasional swim in the summertime. She leaned backward on the rope and shook her head, as if she were trying to shake herself free. We tugged her, step by step, after us, and gradually she became less uneasy.

At the mouth of the cave we stopped. It was horribly dark in there. Surely those were pale, yellow-faced ghosts sitting high up on the walls.

"It's the moonlight on the wet rock," said Pat's voice in my ear, and I knew that he had been as frightened as I.

It is a strange thing that once one has been told that a place is haunted one never really loses the little, uneasy fear of it. Although both Pat and I knew very well that Mike Coffey had invented the story of the Spanish ghosts for the sole purpose of frightening us, still it was with terror in our hearts that we advanced every step.

The darkness seemed impenetrable. We felt the sandy floor of the cave rise under our feet and heard the wash of the little waves breaking at the back.

The little strand was there, as the old woman had promised us. At the water's edge we stopped and looked back toward the mouth of the cave. Its pointed arch and jagged sides were outlined sharply now in the moonlight. And here, marching through the shiny water, came Luke, for the third time carrying the grandmother in his arms. He seemed to have no difficulty in seeing his way through the thick darkness. He walked right past us and set the old woman on her feet on the sand.

" 'Tis the way I'm getting fond of that style of travelling," said she demurely. "You're as good as a horse and buggy, Luke, and that's no lie."

At the top of the strand, sure enough, there was a little piece of soft, dry sand such as is found only above the high-water mark. It was deathly cold, of course, for the sun never came in here. Now that we had become accustomed to the darkness, we noticed that a tiny glow seemed to come from the little line of white at the water's edge. We settled the old woman on a low, flat rock against the back wall of the cave, with the filly as close beside her as we could induce her to go.

"She'll keep you warm, Mrs. Conroy, ma'am," said Luke. "Let the two of ye be telling each other stories until we come back."

Pat and I wanted to take off our jerseys and give them to the old woman to sit on, but she would not allow it. She hustled us out of the cave, urging us to get the pookaun into a safe place as quickly as possible.

When we were out on the strand again, Luke said:
"She's a great old soldier, for certain sure, but she'll get her death of cold inside in that cave if we leave her there for long. A woman that has hardly stirred from the hob for years!"

We wasted no time in talking. Our first task was to move the boat. In her present position, the strong moonlight turned her into a silver boat, picked out in every detail. We shoved her off and jumped aboard her and hauled up sail almost in one movement. Farther along the coast, beyond the valley strand, where we had never been before, we found a huge jumble of black boulders. Wicked reefs put out long fingers to catch us.

"If we strike on one of those," said Luke grimly, "we'll have to walk back to Inishrone."

We had to keep far out to sea and watch our chance until we saw a wide space between the reefs. Then we sailed in and ran aground on a narrow stony beach. Rock-faced cliffs towered over us. We moored the pookaun with a long rope to a rock above the high-water mark. Luke tapped her sharply on the nose.

"No tricks, now!" he said to her. "If you let me down tonight, after all the years we've been together, I'll sell you as surely as there's a tail on a cat!"

The pookaun said never a word.

"To look at her, you'd think butter wouldn't melt in her mouth," said Luke to us as we scrambled along the strand.

A short distance away we found a place where a cascade of loose stones and sand on the sloping cliff's face made it possible for us to climb slowly upward. Luke went in front, carefully testing each foothold to make sure that it was safe. It seemed to me that there had once been a sort of track or path here, which was now covered over with sand. Luke led us at a slant toward the right, so as to make the ascent easier. In this way, when we reached the top of the cliff, we were not far from the cave where the grandmother and the filly lay hidden.

We crawled up on to level ground and lay there for a moment, resting. Then, moving like snakes, we began to drag ourselves forward, so that we could look down into the valley. It was cold up there, with the little sharp teeth of the wind nipping at us continually. Down below us, quite near, the troop of horses moved quietly in and out as they grazed. Out on the edge, as usual, the black stallion kept watch. The strand was almost covered by the tide, and the long waves broke only at the very edge of the water. We listened and heard those same waves booming in the cave below us. I wondered if the old woman was afraid in there, alone with the filly.

"Look!" said Luke's voice in my ear. "The Coffeys!"

There they came, sailing their big hooker in so smoothly and surely that it was plain to be seen that they had often done it before.

"They can't be bringing her in to the strand," said Pat. "She's much too big."

We were all silent then, watching the hooker so intently that I thought my eyes would pop out on stalks, like a snail's. Fifty yards out from the shore they hove to and dropped anchor. In the little quiet interval between waves we heard it splash into the sea. Now we saw that the hooker was trailing a coracle. They hauled it in close and Mike threw a bundle down into it. Then he boarded the coracle with a thump that made it buck like an unbroken horse. Now that the big boat had swung around, we could see the long, stringy shape of Andy, twitching about in fear of getting down from it into the small boat. Though we were too far away to hear, we could imagine how he must be bleating and wailing. We could have told him that he need expect no sympathy from his father. Suddenly he stopped moving for a moment, and then we saw him climb slowly over the side of the hooker and drop into the coracle. Luke gave a short, sour laugh.

"There's one man that should never go to sea," he said. "I wonder what the old man said to him."

Mike was already sending the little boat shooting in to the strand. Silver dripped from the narrow-bladed oars. Andy lay crouched in the stern, and only his thin, flat head showed above the gunwale.

For such a heavy man Mike was surprisingly agile. No sooner had they landed than he slung his bundle over his shoulder, and a moment later he had the coracle turned over and he and Andy were carrying it up the strand to place it above the high-water mark. Then Mike sent Andy scuttling back for the oars. Now that they were so much nearer we could hear his shouts, and Andy's anguished yelps as he jumped to obey.

At these sounds the horses had all lifted their heads to look down toward the shore. Without waiting for Andy, Mike started toward them.

Now, all at once, we saw what he was carrying. He did not touch the wild horses at first, but he went to each one of the others and slipped a headstall over its ears. At the same time he hitched a long rope to the headstall so that he could lead the horse after him. In this way, within a very short time he had a string of horses meekly following him with outstretched necks, one behind the other. Then he placed Andy, as still as a post, holding the leading horse.

"Did you ever see the beat of that?" said Luke in a furious whisper.

"They'll have to wait until the tide goes down to get them out of the valley," said Pat. "I'm sure they'd never try to swim them after the hooker. If one of those horses gave up, he'd sink the whole string."

"If Mike gets away with them," said I, "no one will ever be able to prove that he stole them at all."

"Come on, boys," said Luke sharply. "We're going down into the valley."

Pat hung back.

"What harm if he does get away with them?" he said. "Wouldn't it be a grand ending to the whole story?"

But Luke's hand shot out suddenly to point downward.

"Look at what he's doing now!" he said softly.

Mike had just succeeded in catching a little, dancing,

wild colt, older than the one that we had brought home with us and not quite so pretty. We had noticed this colt because he always galloped with the black stallion and they seemed to enjoy a great many private jokes together. Pat said, with sudden venom:

"Now I know what Stephen Costelloe is planning!"

"Do you tell me so?" said Luke ironically.

"That colt is for him," said Pat with certainty. "When he gets it, he'll tell John to keep the other one. And then he'll never agree to the marriage. I wonder how much Stephen has promised Mike for this colt."

"You may be sure that Mike never sells anything cheap," said Luke. His voice rose. "But I'm thinking he'll have to earn his money hard this time. Look at that!"

As soon as he thought that he had the colt safe, Mike had made the mistake of jerking roughly at his headstall as he led him toward the string of horses. The colt's front feet came up. He shook his head and danced a step or two on his hind legs. Then he let out a long, anguished whinny, in the exact tone of a small boy that shouts for his father when he is in danger.

Immediately the black stallion lifted his head. He had shown no interest in the capture of the string of horses, as if he knew that this was their ordinary fate. But at the cry of the wild colt he threw back his head and bared his teeth silently, in a way that made my blood run cold even at the safe distance of the top of the cliff. Then he began to move, quite slowly, toward Mike, in a curious prancing motion. Mike still struggled with the colt. They circled around each other while Mike tried to drag his head down. Luke stood up and gave a tremendous shout that echoed all around the valley:

"Let him go, you fool! Let him go!"

Then he started to swing down over the precipitous face of the cliff. Some strange inspiration guided his feet into impossible footholds. Craned over the cliff to watch him, it seemed to me and to Pat as if he sometimes clung by sheer strength of will. We glanced across at Mike. He was still obstinately holding on to the colt, which was dragging him frantically about. Still the stallion advanced, still slowly. The moonlight on his satin skin made strange patterns as he moved. His teeth shone like silver in the white light.

"I'm going down, too," said Pat suddenly. "Stay you here, Danny."

And over the top of the cliff he went before I had time to reply. I watched painfully as he moved slowly in Luke's tracks. Once he hung without moving for a minute, so that I was sure he had lost his nerve. But then he went on again, still slower, never looking downward. When at last his feet touched the ground, he lay down on the grass as if he had fallen. I leaned far over the cliff to call to him. Then, with my head reeling, I drew back.

While I had been watching Pat, I had glanced from moment to moment at the extraordinary circus that was going on down in the valley. Now I saw that Luke and Mike were struggling for possession of the colt. The stallion was so close now that I thought they must surely feel his hot breath on them. Andy moved a step forward as if he thought of going to help his father. Then he seemed to change his mind, for after that he stayed there, watching, as if he had grown into the ground like a tree.

Suddenly the stallion squealed. Right beside them as he was, the sound must have been deafening. Now, at last, Mike let go his hold of the colt. Immediately, Luke twitched off the headstall and sent the colt galloping off up the valley with a thundering blow on his ribs. In one gasping breath I let out all the pent up terror that had been suffocating me. I saw Pat leap to his feet and stare fixedly for a moment after the colt. Then he began to run toward the spot where Luke and Mike were still standing. I heard Luke talking softly to the stallion, which still stood by them. The stallion took no notice of him. He stretched forward his splendid arched neck and snapped those terrible teeth an inch from Mike Coffey's ear. Mike's squeal of fear almost matched the stallion's. With only a second to spare, he had drawn back out of reach. Now he began to walk backward, stiff-legged. The stallion came after him, quietly menacing. Mike dared not turn and run. He put out his hands and made a little pushing gesture with them as if he could push the stallion away from him. It was horrible to watch, and I felt myself wither with a kind of primitive fear.

All at once, Pat's clear voice rang out:

"Run, Mike! Run!"

Then Pat was beside the stallion, clutching at its mane. A moment later he had sprung onto that twisting, prancing back and was holding on to the stallion's neck.

Up came its front hooves, pawing the air with temper. Pat slipped a little sideways, but he still held on. Luke clutched at the stallion's tail and pulled with all his might. The stallion came down on all fours again, and then his hind hooves were flying in the air. Luke skipped out of the way. I could see Pat, in the midst of trying to keep his hold, patting the stallion's neck as if they were the best of friends.

"And now, oh, now it's time for me to climb down the face of the cliff," said I to myself in despair.

For here came Mike, trotting like a very old donkey, swaying a little from side to side as if at any moment he might fall. I knew that he was safe only for as long as the stallion was occupied with Pat. But if once Pat lost his grip and fell off, the stallion would come looking for Mike again. Stallions are single-minded beasts, and their memories are long.

Ever since that climb down into the valley I have had a deep respect for cats. Remembering Pat, I did not look downward, but felt with my bare toes until I found each tiny foothold. Then I curled them around whatever projection was supporting me, and heartily I wished that I had long, sharp claws to help me. I fell the last five feet, and in the second before I touched the ground and rolled over I lived an age of despair. Many a night since then, in my dreams, I have passed through those moments again and wakened with a thump in my bed, feeling my limbs anxiously for broken bones.

I had fallen almost at Mike's feet. I could not see his

face clearly in the dim light, but I well remember the way he hunched his shoulders stupidly as he looked at me, as if he had never seen an animal like me before. I think it was the sudden wish to laugh that brought me back to my senses.

I bounded to my feet and clutched at his arm.

"You must hide, hide!" I said. "There's only one place. Come on!"

He hung back.

"What about Andy?"

I had not thought that he would bother about Andy.

"The stallion won't touch Andy," I said, a little more gently. "It's you he's after."

I glanced across to make sure that Pat was still on the stallion's back. Then I trotted Mike down to the strand. He followed me as meekly as a whipped dog. We carried the coracle down to the water's edge at a run, and I launched her while he went back for the oars. We shoved off then, and I gave him only one oar in case he would try to make for his own hooker, instead of following my plan. But it seemed never to occur to him not to do as I told him. I had the bow oar; and as I watched him bend his back tiredly, I saw for the first time that he was an old man.

Along the line of the shore we went and made straight for the end of the cliff. Mike turned his head.

"Watch out!" he said. "She'll be holed if she touches the cliff."

"We're going into the cave," I said. "You'll be well looked after in there."

He made no answer to this. We shipped the oars and eased the boat into the cave with our hands on the cold walls. Then I stepped out into shallow water and hauled her up on the tiny strand. I made out the dark shapes of the grandmother and the filly, moving in the gloom. I could hear the filly's light, quick breathing.

"I have a visitor for you, Mrs. Conroy," I said.

"Who is it, Danny?"

By the sound of her voice, she was rested and happy. Mike was ashore now, too, and he gave a little exclamation of astonishment as he peered into the gloom. I pushed the coracle off again, stern first, and ran into the water after her. She rocked as I got over the side. As I pushed my way out of the cave I called back over my shoulder the answer to the grandmother's question:

"Mr. Michael Coffey!"

At the mouth of the cave I held on for a moment and listened. Away inside, deepened by the echo, I could hear Mrs. Conroy's chuckle as she said:

"Arrah, Mike, agrá, is it yourself that's in it? Come on over here and sit down on the stool, for that's all I have to offer you. I'd make a cup of tay only that the fire is after going out on me—"

I waited for no more but started to row back to the strand.

15

THE END OF THE STORY

I had gone no more than half-way when I heard the sound of a boat's engine. It was a powerful engine, and I recognized it at once. The lifeboat was the only boat in our neighborhood that made a sound like that.

My first instinct was to give one mighty stroke of the oars, sending the coracle like an arrow toward the strand, so that I could warn the others that strangers were coming. In the last few days we had developed such a habit of hiding, and running away, and dodging, and slipping around corners, that I wondered if we would ever again be able to lie straight in bed. Now I realized all at once that I would be very glad indeed to become a mere boy again, instead of a sort of junior gentleman of fortune.

I plunged my oars into the water and stayed there, floating, while I tried to make out whether the boat was coming this way. Then I saw it rounding the end of the cliff from the direction of the island quay. In the light on its masthead I saw a crowd of people on board, all gazing toward the Coffeys' hooker.

I waited until the engine was switched off and then I rowed quickly toward the lifeboat. I did not call out, for there was still Andy to be thought of. As I came alongside, a voice from above my head said:

"Who's that? Answer quickly!"

"It's Danny MacDonagh," I said, for I had recognized Bartley Conroy's voice at once, "and Pat is quite safe, here on the island. At least I think he is," I added doubtfully, as I remembered the position in which I had last seen him.

"Where is my mother?"

"Safe and sound, in a good place."

Now the gunwale was lined with faces. The first one that I saw was my own father. He put up his hand in salute to me, and I replied in the same way. John Conroy was there, too, beside his father. I saw many silver-buttoned overcoats, worn this time by real Guards. One of them said:

"Is Luke the Cats with you too?"

This was the thin Sergeant from Kilmoran. There was no sign of the huge, sleepy one. I supposed that they had left him behind to keep law and order in Kilmoran;

or perhaps they were afraid that he would make the boat list.

"Yes, Luke is here," I said. "He's with Pat this moment. We have Mike Coffey safely put away. You can get him out whenever you want him."

"Put away? Where? Where is he?"

All the Guards became very excited, like beagles on the scent.

"I'll show you, after a while," I said.

Suddenly I was shaking very gently, though I was not cold. John Conroy swung a leg over the gunwale and dropped into the coracle. His father pushed forward and followed him. Then came the Sergeant and my father, and a strange Guard whom I had not seen before, but who, as I discovered later, came from Lettermullen.

I saw that the Dutch captain was in the lifeboat too, pulling away at his pipe as if he were sitting by a kitchen fire on Inishrone. And strangest of all it was to see a Clancy child, a small boy of about eight years, silent as always, peeping unsmilingly down at me into the coracle.

"Move down to the stern, Danny," said John, taking the oars out of my hands. "You've done enough work for one night."

The lifeboat coxswain, Peter Fahy from Rossmore, dropped his anchor then and said he would wait for us. I thought that the five Guards who were left behind looked disappointed. Then we were away from the lifeboat on our way to the strand.

Bartley Conroy was the first ashore. John and I came

after. All three of us pulled the boat up on the sand, so that the two Guards could step ashore without wetting their boots and the ends of their beautiful trousers. But they ran as fast as any of us up the strand to the first ridge of sea grass that cut off our view of the valley.

The night was still bright with moonlight. I had not dared to think of what would be waiting for us. John was the first to see Pat.

"Praises be to God!" he said softly. "Will you look at that for a horse!"

There came Pat, riding slowly toward us on the black stallion's back. Every movement that they made was so complete and harmonious that it seemed as if they shared the same body between them. The stallion arched his neck and swished his tail as he passed us by, where we stood in a little gaping crowd. He stopped for a moment and pawed the ground, as if he were going to dance a minuet. Then he moved on again.

"Good man, Patcheen!" said Bartley with a sudden shout of laughter.

"Please, please don't shout," Pat implored him. The stallion walked on, and we had to follow him to hear the rest. "This fellow is not an ordinary horse. Only that he's worn out from prancing and jumping, he'd never let me sit on him at all. And I'm afraid to get off!"

It was Luke and John between them that halted the stallion. He snapped feebly once, and then he stood there quietly while they held him by the mane. We all gathered around to look at him. Sure enough, he was worn out from struggling with Pat. He cocked a tiredly wicked eye at us and blew softly through his nostrils. Pat slid cautiously to the ground and staggered over to me.

"Don't talk to me of horses for a week, Danny," he said. "Is everything all right in the cave?"

"All fine," said I.

"The cave? What cave? Where's the grandmother?" This was Bartley, suddenly anxious.

"We'll show you now," I said.

But we were delayed for a minute longer in starting, for there came Andy, plodding through the light ground mist, leading his string of horses behind him.

"What am I to do with these horses?" he said querulously. "I'm sick and tired of holding them."

"Ha! Andy Coffey!" said the Sergeant from Kilmoran. "Me love to you! *I'll* take charge of the horses for you!"

And he picked the leading rein out of Andy's hand and presented it to his companion to hold.

Then we all went down to the Coffeys' coracle.

"You can stay here with the horses," said the Sergeant from Kilmoran to the Lettermullen man. "The rest of us will go in the boat—Luke the Cats, Bartley Conroy, John Conroy, Danny MacDonagh, James MacDonagh, Pat Conroy—"

"You're like the schoolmaster calling the roll, Sergeant," said Luke. " 'Twould make a cat laugh to listen to you, so it would. If we all get into the coracle there won't be room for the passengers that we must pick up in the cave."

So the Sergeant left it to Luke to settle who would

go. In the end, only the two of themselves went, and
Bartley Conroy, because he wanted to make sure as
quickly as possible that his mother was safe. He had
not said anything to us about what we had done with
her, but somehow we were glad not to be too near him
for a while. Neither of us wanted to visit the cave again,
and we felt quite safe in leaving the next part of the
business to Luke.

When the coracle was gone, my father began to ask
us questions. Our answers were so wild, however, that
he soon gave up. We were as hungry as scald crows, for
we had not eaten for hours. The good food that we had
brought with us was around in the pookaun, at the other
side of the cliff. Neither of us could even think of scaling
that cliff, even to get at the food. My father guessed
what was wrong with us, and he milked a whole bag of
bull's-eyes from the Lettermullen Guard who was holding the horses. He gave them up willingly enough, to
give him his due.

Then my father made us run up and down on the
sand, so that we would not get chilled, he said. It was
John Conroy who put a stop to this. He said that if we
did not take life easy, we would be so worn out that it
would hardly be worth anyone's while to bring us home.

Presently we saw the coracle come back slowly from
the cave and go toward the lifeboat. John Conroy and
my father gazed at it through the darkness.

"Why is Luke the Cats hanging out over the stern?"
my father asked after a moment.

"We forgot to say that we had a little wild filly inside

in the cave with the grandmother," I said. "I suppose they have her swimming after the coracle now, and that Luke is holding her chin above water with his hands."

We went down to the edge of the sea to see how they would manage to get the filly onto the lifeboat. It seemed not to be too difficult. They had a little machine on board that was usually used for hoisting shipwrecked sailors out of the water. It served equally well with the filly. Then the Sergeant and Luke and Bartley all came back in the coracle to fetch us. They brought a Rossmore Guard with them.

It was arranged that the two Guards would spend the rest of the night on the island. The Sergeant promised to send out a big boat the next day to take the string of stolen horses in to Galway. He gave the men bread and cheese and chocolate to eat during their wait. They did not like it, but they could not complain.

The lifeboat brought us around to Luke's pookaun. She was floating now on the risen tide, and she seemed to have waited patiently enough. Luke never doubted that we would be willing to sail with him. Neither of us dared to tell him that we feared his boat was not as seaworthy as the lifeboat. When John Conroy offered to come in the pookaun, too, we felt a little easier. Peter Fahy gave us a big lantern to hang on the mast.

The grandmother was sitting comfortably in a sheltered place on the lifeboat, smiling to herself and holding a drink in her hand. She gave us a beautiful, broad wink, but she said nothing. Out of the tail of my eye, I saw Mike Coffey and Andy standing together watching us. In spite of their sins, I felt a surge of sympathy for them. I was glad when the lifeboat got under way again and ticked off into the darkness. Its lantern swayed gently up and down as it rode the waves.

When it had gone out of sight, Luke gave a long, satisfied sigh.

"I don't know about the rest of ye," said he, "but I could do with a fine sleep." He laughed shortly. "Ha! Did you see the old woman, with a smile on her like a cat in a tripe shop? She's not a bit the worse for her night out."

We cast off then and followed in the wake of the lifeboat. Luke was pleased to have John on board, and he spent the first few minutes in pointing out to him what an excellent pookaun she was. Meanwhile Pat and I had found the soda-bread and were sending it to a speedy end. Though John was bursting with curiosity, he was too polite to cut Luke short. Presently, however, Luke himself brought the talk back to the evening's adventure by saying:

" 'Tis a sin and a shame to leave that island go to waste. Ye should breed horses there, the way 'twas done in the olden times. But don't go bringing that stallion off the island. 'Twould break his black heart, so it would. Who owns the Island of Horses now, anyway?"

"It belongs to us, I suppose," said John. "Everyone from the island went to Portland in America after the disaster. Only my grandmother stayed at home on Inish-rone, and she got married. There might be people in Portland with a claim on it, but I'd say they wouldn't be bothered with it. If we breed horses here," he finished thoughtfully, "I can stop lamenting over the black colt that Stephen Costelloe is to get."

"You're not going to give him the colt now, after he tried to cheat you by getting another one?" said Luke indignantly.

"I'll have to, for Barbara's sake," said John. "Besides, Stephen hardly knows when he is cheating now, he's so used to it. Barbara's mother is a grand, hearty sort of a woman. I often wonder how she came to marry a person like Stephen."

Luke snorted.

"If the cat had cows, he'd get an offer of marriage. I'm not saying she married him for his money," he added hastily. "I was thinking more like that her people made a match for her with Stephen and maybe thought they were doing well for her."

Pat and I nearly smothered with swallowing our laughter at the way in which all of Luke's proverbs and sayings had to do with cats.

After that we had to tell John every single thing that had happened to us, from our abduction by Foxy and Joe until the moment when the lifeboat arrived at the Island of Horses. In return, he told us how the Clancy child that we had seen on the lifeboat had overheard the elder Miss Doyle talking over the telephone to Mike Coffey and telling him that we had set off in the pookaun with the grandmother. Like everyone else on Inishrone, Miss Doyle had made the mistake of thinking that because the Clancy child seldom spoke he could not hear. He had run at once to The Suit of Sails, where all the men were gathered. He had tugged at Bartley's coat-tails until he had got his attention. Then he had whispered the information that had started the lifeboat on our track. A ride in the same lifeboat had been his reward. It was the sight of Mike's hooker, anchored off the strand, that had brought them in there.

"But why did Miss Doyle come to spy on us and then tell Mike Coffey?" I asked. "I can see now that Foxy and Joe had been in with her, too. But I don't see why she should have to do with those blackguards."

"We got that out of her before we left," said John. "She said that Mike had promised to get her transferred to a mainland post office. He made out that he was a very powerful man and had only to ask for a favor like that to get it. Mike has been using the Island of Horses for several years past, she says. He used to bring stolen horses there and leave them until the hue and cry about them would have died down. He was always afraid that the Inishrone people would find out what he was at. Miss Doyle always told him if she thought that anyone had been near it. She was suffering from terrible remorse when we set out. That's why your mother, Danny, and mine couldn't come with us. Comforting Miss Doyle they were, if you please, telling her how much we all love her, and she promising to be good in the future. She even said that she'd put a half-door on the house, so that everyone can walk in and out neighborlike. The sister looked as if she'd like that. I'm thinking the old one holds her down a good bit."

The eastern sky was beginning to brighten by the time we reached Garavin quay. The lifeboat had got there long before us, of course, and everyone on the island seemed to have come to welcome us. By this time Pat and I were staggering from lack of sleep. We were very glad to be bundled into a sidecar and driven home to bed.

For all Luke's talk of sleep, he did not come with us. IIe went up to The Suit of Sails with the men and ate a huge meal of cold potatoes and sour milk, provided by Matt Faherty. He and Matt found that they had a lot in common, and from that day onward they became fast friends.

The next morning the Conroys went to Rossmore. Pat went, too, and it was he who told me how Stephen Costelloe admitted that he was the meanest man in the three parishes and even promised Barbara a dowry of twenty cows and their calves on her marriage.

We could not make Luke understand that Barbara was not in the least like her father. He kept shaking his head over a fine man like John being thrown away on a girl with such a bad drop in her.

"What would the cat's son do but to kill a mouse?" said Luke.

But on his way back to Kilmoran he called at Rossmore to see her, and, just as we expected, after that he could never find words good enough to describe her. He came to the wedding, and sang a wonderful long ballad that he had composed about her.

Mike Coffey went to jail for a while for stealing

horses from stud farms. Andy did not go to jail, for no one thought it worth while to send him there. According to Luke, he spent his time in bringing in little bags of sweets to his father. When Mike came out, they changed their way of living. They set up shop in an inland town, in Tipperary, where Mike got a great reputation as a knowledgeable seafaring man. He never mentioned horses.

So Pat was able to start the wool business after all, and the good times really did come to Inishrone and to many other islands along our coast as well.

The grandmother never left home again. All day long she would sit on the hob, smiling happily to herself every time she thought of her excursion. But she never spoke of it except to me and to Pat, and even then she always waited until we were alone. The beautiful shawl was ruined, all covered with green slime from the cave walls and spotted with sea water. But she did not mind. As she said herself, now that she had gone once more to the Island of Horses she would not be needing it again.

EILÍS DILLON (1920–1994) wrote more than thirty books for young people, as well as fiction for adults, including the best-selling historical novel *Across the Bitter Sea*, about the struggle for Irish independence in the nineteenth and twentieth centuries. With few exceptions, her young people's books are set in the west of Ireland, in small communities struggling to make a living on the islands and along the the Atlantic coast. As the critic Declan Kiberd wrote in Dillon's obituary: "What Laura Ingalls Wilder did for children's literature in the US, she achieved in Ireland, imparting a sure historical sense in books such as *The Singing Cave*. That interest in history was a natural expression of her curiosity of mind, and of her family inheritance."

Building on a family tradition of agitation for Irish independence (her mother's brother was one of seven men who signed the Proclamation of the Irish Republic and was executed by the British at the end of the 1916 Easter Rising), Eilís Dillon committed herself to preserving and promoting Irish literature and culture. She was a Fellow of the Royal Society of Literature and a member and strong supporter of Aosdána, the national association of writers, artists, and composers. She even wrote a few of her children's books in Gaelic, the native Irish language. But, as Kiberd explains, "There was nothing narrowly provincial in her writing: she simply assumed that books about children in Irish settings, if properly written, would be of universal appeal. And so they have proved to be."

TITLES IN SERIES